"Dynamite!"

Drew gave a low whistle. "I always knew that under your clothes there was a fantastic body."

Chrissie's face warmed with pleasure, and the expression in his eyes was making her feel more breathless than ever. The situation was fast getting out of control. "I'll go change into something more modest," she said primly. "You can wait in the library."

"I'd rather go swimming with you," Drew said.

Chrissie lifted her eyebrows. "And what do you propose to wear? Your birthday suit?"

"Why not?" he countered, grinning wickedly. "It's a private pool. You could discard those absurdly tiny strips of cloth you optimistically call a bathing suit and we could skinny-dip. It could be a lot of fun."

"Tempting as your suggestion is," Chrissie said dryly, "I think I'll pass. Skinny-dipping could create a dangerous situation."

Drew's grin widened. "I'm pinning my hopes on just that."

Dear Reader,

Welcome to Silhouette—experience the magic of the wonderful world where two people fall in love. Meet heroines that will make you cheer for their happiness, and heroes (be they the boy next door or a handsome, mysterious stranger) who will win your heart. Silhouette Romance reflects the magic of love—sweeping you away with books that will make you laugh and cry, heartwarming, poignant stories that will move you time and time again.

In the coming months we're publishing romances by many of your all-time favorites, such as Diana Palmer, Brittany Young, Sondra Stanford and Annette Broadrick. Your response to these authors and our other Silhouette Romance authors has served as a touchstone for us, and we're pleased to bring you more books with Silhouette's distinctive medley of charm, wit and—above all—*romance*.

I hope you enjoy this book and the many stories to come. Experience the magic!

Sincerely,

Tara Hughes
Senior Editor
Silhouette Books

SONDRA STANFORD

Proud
Beloved

Published by Silhouette Books New York

America's Publisher of Contemporary Romance

With love for Rhonda and Gregory

SILHOUETTE BOOKS
300 E. 42nd St., New York, N.Y. 10017

ISBN: 0-373-08646-6

First Silhouette Books printing May 1989

Books by Sondra Stanford

Silhouette Romance

Golden Tide #6
Shadow of Love #25
Storm's End #35
No Trespassing #46
Long Winter's Night #58
And Then Came Dawn #88
Yesterday's Shadow #100
Whisper Wind #112
Tarnished Vows #131
Stolen Trust #530
Heart of Gold #586
Proud Beloved #646

Silhouette Special Edition

Silver Mist #7
Magnolia Moon #37
Sun Lover #55
Love's Gentle Chains #91
The Heart Knows Best #161
For All Time #187
A Corner of Heaven #210
Cupid's Task #248
Bird in Flight #292
Equal Shares #326
Through All Eternity #445

SONDRA STANFORD

is a fourth-generation native Texan, and many of her novels are set in her beloved state, although she enjoys traveling elsewhere in search of fresh locales for her books. Sondra believes that love *is* life and she tries to reflect that philosophy in her work.

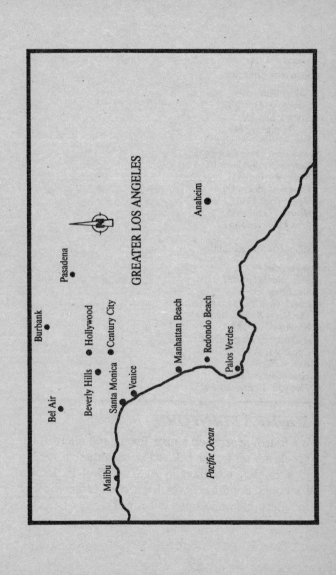

Chapter One

"You know we'd love to have you come with us to Colorado, but I'll admit the Bahamas sound more exciting. The beaches are probably littered with handsome young men." Jack Barrows's eyes twinkled as he looked at his daughter. "Old fuddy-duddies like your mom and me can't hope to compete with an attraction like that!"

"Oh, I don't know," Christina shot back. "I'll bet none of them would be as good-looking as my daddy."

"Humph." Jack adjusted his dark-rimmed eyeglasses and gave Christina one of his sharp, knowing, fatherly looks. "You'll need to get up pretty early in the morning to put such nonsense over me, young lady! You must be looking for a favor. What is it this time...your car need an oil change, or are you wanting me to move something heavy for you again?"

Chrissie chuckled, and her soft blue eyes sparkled with laughter. "Relax. It's neither. Can't I compliment you sometimes without having an ulterior motive?"

Jack grinned. "It's never happened before that I can recall. When you were little, I always knew you were about to ask for something whenever you started with the compliments."

"I must've been about as subtle as mud!"

"That was about the size of it, *chérie*." Marie Barrows entered the room with a dish towel in her hand. "When you were about ten, you told me I was a hundred times nicer than Sally Broussard's mom. Then you asked if we could take one of the puppies Mrs. Broussard was trying to give away, because I was bound to be so nice to the poor creature."

Chrissie laughed. "No wonder I didn't get it! My students are wily little imps who keep trying to throw dust in my eyes, too. I really have to be alert to stay ahead of them." Changing the subject, she said, "The chicken casserole smells delicious, Mom. When do we eat? I'm starving."

"I think it needs to bake a little while longer." Marie sat down in her favorite easy chair. "How does it feel to be free as the breeze for three months?"

"Blissful. I may sleep through the entire summer vacation."

Chrissie closed her eyes and settled deeper into her chair. Her golden-red hair billowed against the cushion, forming a bright halo around her oval face as she sighed, slipped off her white pumps and stretched her long, slender stockinged legs.

It was the first Friday in June, the last day of school for Chrissie and her third-grade students, and she was luxuriating in a sense of glorious freedom. The entire week had been chaotic because the warm, sunny New Orleans weather was far more appealing to the children than their lessons. Somehow Chrissie had hung on, doing her best to maintain some small degree of discipline and order these past few days, but now the difficult time was over—the children were released from the imprisoning classroom at last, and so was she. By September, though, she knew from experience that she would be eager to get back to teaching a whole new crop of bright young minds.

"What's this about the Bahamas?" Marie asked.

Chrissie opened her eyes and exchanged an amused glance with her father. Just because she happened to be busy in the kitchen didn't mean Marie ever missed anything that went on in the living room. She'd heard every word.

"A couple of the other teachers from school are going there on vacation next week, and they invited me along."

"You don't seem very enthused about it."

Chrissie shrugged. "It takes money to get that enthused. I'd like to go, but I don't see how I can afford it. You know how much I've been out this year on my car alone. Only last month I bought four new tires."

"Then you'll be coming with us to Colorado?"

Jack and Marie were planning to drive to Estes Park for their own summer vacation in another week.

"I'm not sure. Catherine Voisin offered me a part-time job in her gift shop for the summer. I suppose I ought to be sensible and accept it. At least it would buy my clothes for the fall term."

"She could do without you for a couple of weeks, surely," Jack said. "You need a little break, honey. Everybody does. If you can't swing the Bahamas, come with us. It might not be as exciting as going away with your friends, but at least it wouldn't cost you anything."

Chrissie smiled. "Thanks, Dad. I'll think about it."

Jack nodded, glanced at the wall clock above the sofa and announced, "Time for the evening news." He made a move to get up from his recliner chair so that he could turn on the television.

Chrissie waved him back. "I'll do it. I'm going to the kitchen to pour myself a glass of tea, anyway." She unwound herself from her chair and crossed the room to the television set.

When she started to leave the room, Marie called from behind her, "Check on the casserole while you're there."

"Sure, Mom."

Chrissie took her time in the kitchen, pouring her tea, checking on the chicken and opening a can of food for her mother's cat, who had begun to meow demandingly when he saw her.

Beauty was a large fuzzy gray cat who had moved in to rule the Barrows household seven years before, the same day eighteen-year-old Chrissie had gone off to college. As Marie had explained it, getting a pet had been absolutely essential for her sanity, something young to cuddle and love and satisfy her maternal nature. From that time on, Chrissie had teased her mother that Beauty was far more spoiled than she, their only child, had ever been.

With regal dignity, Beauty walked over to his bowl and began to eat delicately, without so much as acknowledging Chrissie's efforts on his behalf. "You're such a snob," she told him.

She threw the empty can away and went to the sink to wash the spoon. As usual, her mother's ivy hanging at the window looked thirsty. Chrissie gave it a drink of water and picked off a few dead leaves. That done, she picked up her glass of tea and returned to the living room. "The chicken is—"

"Shh!"

Both her parents hushed her abruptly, their eyes and entire attention focused on the television screen.

Silenced, Chrissie looked at it, too. A photograph of a famous beautiful redhead was displayed behind the newscaster's right shoulder. "Laura Douglas, the actress who won an Oscar for her performance in *Dove's Wings* died today in a tragic accident. She was working on her current film, *The Whirlwind*, when she fell from a piece of scaffolding on the set. Miss Douglas was the widow of the late Martin Timms, the oil industrialist. The couple had no children. She was forty-six."

Following the announcement, the network presented film clips of scenes from several of the actress's movies, but Chrissie was no longer watching the television screen. She was looking from one parent to the other, puzzled over their incomprehensible, compelling interest in the news of the untimely death of a Hollywood actress. Chrissie had probably seen every one of Laura Douglas's movies herself and had admired her beauty and talent, and certainly the word of her death was saddening, but it was hardly the kind of news that would stun her parents into speechlessness. Why, they rarely even went to a movie!

When the segment covering the career highlights of Laura Douglas ended, Marie quietly got up, went to the television set and switched it off. For a long moment she stood there as though uncertain, and then she looked at her husband. Chrissie turned to look at him, too, and her father's face was unusually grave. His earlier relaxed, jovial mood was gone.

"What *is* it?" Chrissie demanded with rising alarm.

Her father exchanged another long look with her mother. Then heavily he said, "It's time."

Marie nodded. "Yes."

"Sit," Jack ordered gruffly. "Both of you sit down."

Marie returned to her chair and sank down abruptly, as though all the wind had been knocked out of her. Chrissie studied her expression intently, trying to decipher it. Something important had just happened here, something she didn't comprehend. Her mother's brunette complexion, normally so rich and vibrant, had turned a sickly sallow color. When Chrissie glanced at her father again, she saw that every feature of his face was strained as though he was under a tremendous emotional pressure.

Jack waved his hand impatiently toward the sofa, once again indicating he wanted Chrissie to sit down. She obeyed, still holding her forgotten glass of iced tea.

A silence fell and both Marie and Jack seemed to be waiting for the other to begin speaking. Their strange behavior brought a chill of alarm to Chrissie. Her throat tightened, and though she was sure she couldn't have made a sound of her own just then, conversely she felt dangerously close to screaming with impatience over their mysterious behavior. As the silence continued, an awful foreboding welled up inside her. They had a secret, a secret she knew instinctively she didn't want to hear, a secret that was going to be unpleasant.

Jack leaned forward in his chair, his dark gaze focused on Chrissie. "Honey..." His voice was raspy. "Christina, honey, that woman...Laura Douglas...was your mother."

At first Chrissie merely stared at him, not absorbing the words. Her mind seemed to float free, high above her, above the tense little family scene, and it was as though her father had not spoken. Then she blinked her eyes, met his penetrating gaze and tried to swallow as the meaning of the words crashed over her mind like a hurricane assaulting the vulnerable low-lying Louisiana coast.

Marie reached out and removed the glass of tea from Chrissie's limp grasp. "Did you hear him, Chrissie?"

Chrissie nodded, bobbing her head.

Jack left his chair and came to sit beside her on the sofa. He draped an arm around her quivering shoulders and took one of her cold hands in his. "We always knew we'd have to tell you someday—that it was only fair to you. But somehow the right time just never came."

"We always thought one day you'd want to search for your natural mother. We planned to tell you as soon as you expressed an interest, if you were old enough to handle the truth. But you never did."

Chrissie shook her head and squeezed her eyes to hold back sudden tears. At last she found her voice in anger. "I never wanted to know anything about the person who gave me away. I wish I still didn't know," she ended on a bitter note. "I wish you hadn't told me now."

"Don't say that!" Marie cried. "Surely it's a relief to know the truth, isn't it?"

Chrissie turned to gaze at her mother—the only mother she'd ever known. The features were still the same—short dark hair, brilliant brown eyes, a cute nose a bit too small for her face and, when she smiled, the sweetest, friendliest smile in the world. *This* . . . this was her mother.

"That woman wasn't my mother," she declared in an unsteady voice. "She may have given birth to me, but she was *never* my mother. She was busy becoming rich and famous while you were baking me Christmas cookies or helping me with my homework or pampering me when I had the chicken pox. No," she added more firmly, "that glitzy movie queen wasn't my mother."

"We don't want you to feel like that, *chérie*," Jack said gently. "We don't want you to hate her or her memory."

"Are you kidding, Dad?" Chrissie's eyebrows raised. "How can you hate what you've never known? I don't hate her. It's just that she never existed for me. She was only a face I saw at the movies once in a while, and that's more than she ever knew of me. I didn't exist for her at all."

"That's not true!" Marie exclaimed. "You existed for her, all right, and I've saved all her letters to prove it. They're in a box in our bedroom closet." She half rose from her chair.

"Let it be until after dinner," Jack said quietly. "Chrissie has plenty of time to read them later."

"What letters?" Chrissie asked, curious in spite of herself. "To me?"

"No. To your father and me," Marie replied. "She wrote every month asking how you were, how we were."

"And your mother always wrote back, telling her about things you were doing and sending her snapshots of you."

Chrissie was astounded. "You corresponded with her all this time? Yet she never wanted to see me or communicate with me?"

"We all agreed it was in your best interest for her not to associate with you," Jack explained. "Any personal involvement could have brought about complications and confusion for you, so she signed an agreement to that effect at the lawyer's office, and in return, we promised to keep her up-to-date on your life."

Marie nodded. "Of course, since she knew our address, in reality Laura could have come to see you at any time and made trouble if she'd chosen to, but she was honorable and kept her word. She genuinely didn't want you to be hurt any more than we did, so she stayed completely out of your life."

"Well, almost." Jack grinned wryly. "She paid for your college education, Chrissie."

"What?" Chrissie raised a trembling hand to her forehead. The shock of the revelations had brought on the beginnings of a headache.

"After she began to make good money, she always wanted to do something for us, for you, but we turned her down. We may not be rich or live in a place like Bel Air, but we got along just fine and we didn't want any of her money. But she really wanted to do something special for you, and since she couldn't send you gifts without rousing your curiosity about who they came from, we finally agreed to allow her to pay for your education. She cared about what happened to you, honey, so we felt like we had to let her do something. After all, she gave us everything when she entrusted you to us!"

"You actually knew her personally?"

"We only met her twice," Jack said. "Both times at the attorney's office. The first time, it was so she could interview us herself and make up her mind about what sort of people we were. The second time was when she signed the adoption papers and gave you to us. She wasn't a famous star then. She was only a scared young woman going through a difficult time."

"Why…" Chrissie's voice was trembling. "Why are you telling me all this now? She's gone. Why didn't you just keep my mother's identity a secret forever?"

"Because of her death," Marie answered gently. "Don't you see? Laura was a wealthy woman, and she was a widow with no other children. Since she knew your adoptive family and where you could be reached, she may have left you something in her will. In case that happens, we didn't want you to hear this news for the first time from a complete stranger."

"Chrissie's heard enough of this matter for the moment," Jack declared firmly. "Let's eat dinner."

The deluge was unrelenting as Andrew Casey drove his rental car from the airport into the city on Thursday afternoon. Drew hunched forward over the steering wheel, peering intently through the solid gray sheet of rain, struggling to read the road signs. If he missed his exit, it would be the crowning touch to an already perfectly lousy day.

A couple of years ago he'd visited New Orleans with some buddies during Mardi Gras and had a marvelous time, but today was different. This time he was here on business, and the hot, muggy, rain-soaked June afternoon was not at all to his liking. He'd have given much to still be in sunny California.

To his relief, Drew spotted his exit, dropped off the freeway and drove to the downtown hotel where he had a res-
ervation.

Twenty minutes later he was inside his hotel room with a
city map spread out before him on the bed. He ought to attend now to the business he'd come for, he supposed, while
it was still daylight. But he was tired and in a bad mood, and
he had no desire to venture back out into that torrential
downpour. No harm would come from letting things hang
until tomorrow, by which time hopefully the storm would
be over.

That decision made, Drew stripped off his clothes down
to his briefs. He caught sight of himself in the dresser mirror but was unimpressed with what he saw, although his
image wasn't bad at all. He was thirty-one, with dark brown
hair, intelligent brown eyes and a finely chiseled jaw. In addition he was well over six feet tall, nicely built with powerful shoulders and thighs, and his skin was bronzed, since
he spent much of his free time outdoors. When he'd been
younger, he'd won a football scholarship to UCLA and his
career on the playing field had been good enough that later
he'd been offered a draft with a pro-football team. It had
been tempting, but he'd had personal doubts that he was
that good, so he'd chosen instead to work his way through
law school.

Turning his back on his nearly naked reflection, Drew
swept the New Orleans city map from the bed and flopped
down on the mattress in its place. Since he probably hadn't
taken an afternoon nap since the age of three, he was du-
bious about his ability to actually fall asleep, but out of
sheer boredom it was worth a try. At least it was more appealing than watching soap operas on TV or floating around
outside in all that rain.

The day had started off badly and had continued to slide
downhill. He'd overslept because he'd forgotten to set his

alarm the night before, and then he'd had trouble locating his stash of traveler's checks before leaving the apartment. Once he'd boarded the plane, it was only to sit there and fume for an hour while the flight was delayed due to mechanical troubles. That hadn't done a thing for any of the passengers' confidence or morale. Finally they'd arrived in New Orleans an hour and a half late only to be greeted by a flood. Did it always rain like this here? he wondered. All he knew for sure was that he'd have done better to rent Noah's ark instead of a car.

Drew crossed his arms behind his head and stared at the ceiling. Well…here he was, feeling more like an errand boy than a practicing attorney. At least he knew where to contact this one, he comforted himself, but who knew how long it would take to find the second one, if ever? He was apt to spend a major portion of the next five years of his life working on this case.

He guessed he shouldn't complain. He was fortunate to have a job with such a prestigious firm as Pitts, Smythe and Raleigh. The senior partners were only being fair when they gave the meatier, more interesting assignments to the attorneys with more experience and seniority. Drew had a healthy respect for fair play and knew he wasn't being ill-treated. It was only that he preferred to actually practice law, to have a case he could sink his teeth into, and instead he had turned into a messenger boy and private detective rolled into one.

The private detective part might be fun, he mused, if he was tracking down something or someone involved in a criminal case à la Perry Mason. But finding a missing person for an estate inheritance? Dull. Dull. Dull.

Drew draped one arm across his eyes to block out the gray light that came from the window and he sighed. *Be honest,* he told himself. *None of those considerations are what really bothers you, and you know it.*

He'd been in a more-or-less permanent rotten mood for months now, and the truth was that almost anything could ignite his short fuse—the fact that there was no milk in the refrigerator when he wanted a bowl of cereal, that the laundry put too much starch in his shirt collars, that his younger brother, David, and Susan, his new bride of three months, were lovey-dovey and much too happy.

Especially that. Until last week when his mother had insisted that Drew attend a family dinner, he'd managed to avoid seeing them ever since their wedding. That night he'd chatted companionably with his older brother, Bruce, and his wife, but it had been all he could do to be civil to David and Susan, fond as he was of them both. Their joy was a slap in his face, and though he'd tried to bury it beneath the surface, his mother knew. After dinner she had taken Drew aside privately and given him a little lecture. "Some things just don't work out, son, but *all* things eventually work out for the best. Remember that, and don't begrudge your brother. Envy will poison you…and your relationship with David, too, if you're not careful. You hardly spoke two words to him tonight and don't think he didn't notice. He's hurt, Drew, and he's not guilty of anything."

It was probably the harshest lecture his mother had given him since he'd been a teenager, released from a night at a juvenile shelter after he'd gone along with some destructive pranks. She'd been so disappointed in him then that Drew had made a silent vow never again to give her cause to be ashamed of him. But his distancing himself from David had brought her fresh heartache, and Drew had been ashamed again.

Sighing, Drew left the bed and went to the window. It might be his imagination, but it seemed as though the rainstorm was less ferocious than before.

At least he'd straightened things out with his brother, he thought as he gazed at the swirling raindrops on the windowpane. The very next day he'd gone to see David and been open and honest with him. His resentment had stemmed from pain and embarrassment, as well as an un-avoidable envy. Thank God, Dave had understood and readily accepted his apology. Drew couldn't have lived with himself if he'd permanently alienated his brother.

His gaze became unfocused as he allowed his thoughts to progress from Dave to Carol. He supposed she was married to her old geezer by now. Even after four months he couldn't think of Carol and that man without getting a sick feeling in his stomach. The heartache was gone now; so was any love he'd once believed he'd felt for her. She had killed that emotion just as surely as a bullet in his heart would have killed his body. But self-condemnation remained...for being such a fool as to care for her in the first place, for misread-ing her character so completely.

Drew and Carol had planned a double wedding with Dave and Susan, but only a month before the date they had set, Carol had broken their engagement. It had been a big enough blow to him that she hadn't really loved him, that she'd actually been two-timing him, but when she'd told him the entire story, his ego had been flattened. The man she intended to marry was sixty-two years old, a grandfather no less, but he had money, barrels of it, and apparently he was willing to spend it all on her. Marrying an up-and-coming attorney had been good enough when it was the best she could do for herself, but when Carol had discovered she could do better, Drew hadn't stood a chance. Carol hadn't even tried to hide the fact that she was marrying the other man for money.

As if that weren't enough, Drew had also had to suffer the excruciating embarrassment of his brother's wedding... the same ceremony that originally had been meant to his and Carol's wedding, too. He'd known full well that everyone present that day was pitying him. It had been the most horrible day of his life, and his pride was still battered and bruised by the ordeal.

The rain was definitely lessening. Drew turned back to the room and began to put on his clothes once more. He might as well try to accomplish what he'd come here to do. If he could get his assignment out of the way this evening, he'd be able to catch a flight back to L.A. tomorrow.

The task ahead wasn't one he could conjure up any enthusiasm for. He was about to make a young woman of twenty-five very happy, very happy indeed, by announcing to her that she was heir to millions of dollars, but the very notion of it just naturally put a bad taste in his mouth. Rationally he understood that Carol had colored his feelings with resentment. Even so, he couldn't shake off his peevish ill humor.

"Hi. You think it might rain today, or what?"

Chrissie laughed, picked up the telephone from the table and carried it to the sofa where she sat down. "How're you doing, Jim? I haven't heard from you in ages."

"You know how it is. I've been busy."

"Yeah. What's her name?"

"Her name is Penny, but I'm not busy anymore."

"It figures. Would you be calling me otherwise?"

Jim Everett chuckled. "You know me like a book."

"When you've known someone for about twenty years, I should hope so."

Jim groaned. "You make us sound so old."

Chrissie sighed. "We're definitely beyond playground stage, pal."

Chrissie and Jim had been friends since their grammar school days. They'd graduated from high school together and both attended LSU in Baton Rouge at the same time. After college they'd both returned to New Orleans, she to teach school, he to work for a television station as a news reporter. These days they only kept up with each other occasionally, when one or the other was in between romances, which in Jim's case was rare.

"How about a movie tonight?" he suggested.

"In this weather? You've got to be kidding! I intend to stay nice and dry and cuddle up with a book. Ask me again when we don't need a pirogue to get there."

"Hmm. Maybe you're right," Jim conceded. "It's just that I'm..."

"At loose ends," Chrissie laughingly finished for him.

"Right. And there's nothing good on TV tonight, and I forgot to rent a new video."

"Poor Jim. You really are lost without a girlfriend at the ready, aren't you?"

"Hmm. Enough about my love life. How's yours doing? Got a new man in your life?"

"Not at the moment. Finding out I had another mother has been more than enough for me."

"What're you talking about?" Jim asked. "You always knew you were adopted."

"Yes, but it never seemed real as long as I didn't know her identity."

"You didn't tell me you were trying to trace your real mother. Or did she track you down?"

"It turns out she always knew where I was. Hang on to your hat, Jim. My real mother was none other than Laura Douglas."

There was a startled silence. "*The* Laura Douglas?"

"That's the one."

Jim's shrill whistle pierced Chrissie's ear. "You wouldn't pull my leg about a thing like that, would you?"

"Do you hear me laughing?"

"Well, can you beat that? Tell me everything."

Chrissie told him what few details she knew herself, finding it a relief to talk with a good friend. For nearly a week she'd kept everything bottled inside. As she talked, her gaze fell on a cardboard box on the floor, next to a potted schefflera. It was the box of letters from Laura that Marie had saved all these years. So far Chrissie had not been able to bring herself to open it.

"Wasn't her funeral held a couple of days ago?" Jim asked. "Did you go?"

"The news reports said the private services were arranged by her friends and attended by invitation only. Since I wasn't a close friend, I suppose I wasn't important enough to be invited." Chrissie couldn't quite keep the bitterness from her voice. She'd felt so strange to be sitting before her television set, listening to a reporter in Los Angeles saying those words the day of her own mother's funeral. It had made her feel unreal, as though she were a nonentity.

"Maybe the friends didn't know about you," Jim said in an obvious effort to comfort her.

"Maybe. Anyway, I wouldn't have gone if I *had* been invited. She was a stranger to me. She didn't want me in her life while she was alive, so why would she have wanted me there when..."

The doorbell rang, interrupting her.

"I've got to go, Jim. Can you believe someone's at the door in weather like this? Call me again sometime about the movie, okay?"

"Sure. And hey...don't let that business about Laura Douglas get you down. At least now you know in your own mind who your mother actually was. You'll never have to wonder again. And look on the bright side—she was nothing short of gorgeous right up to the last, so you can be pretty certain your own looks will still be there when you reach *your* forties!"

"Silly." She smiled in amusement. Jim had succeeded after all in making her laugh. "Bye, Jim."

The doorbell rang a second time as Chrissie hung up the phone. "Coming," she called.

A moment later she opened the door. A man she'd never seen before, who was probably in his early thirties, stood there. He was wearing a soggy gray suit and he was dripping on the doormat. Dark brown hair was plastered to his head, and droplets of water gave a sheen to his face. A rather nice face, she noticed, in spite of its disgruntled expression. Deep brown eyes reflected the man's damp misery.

"Miss Barrows? Christina Barrows?"

"Yes?"

"I'm Andrew Casey, an attorney with the law firm of Pitts, Smythe and Raleigh in Los Angeles, California. I have something of importance to discuss with you. Would you mind if I came inside to do it? It's awfully wet out here."

Something cold curled inside Chrissie, snaking around her heart like an icy hand. The sheltered security she'd always known within the loving care of her adoptive parents had slipped badly this past week. Ever since learning the truth about her mother's identity, she'd felt disoriented, unsettled and uncertain. All her life the question of her true identity had been there, buried and ignored in her subconscious, but never far from her in reality. As she'd grown older, she'd been aware that many adoptive children attempted to locate their natural parents. She had fled in the opposite direction, obstinately settling the matter in her own mind with the assurance that she didn't ever want to know. Marie and Jack Barrows had given her everything a child needed, and Chrissie had wanted nothing of a mother who had given her away like last year's discarded clothes. Learning her mother was someone as famous and wealthy as Laura Douglas had only compounded the pain of that knowledge. She had been worthless to her mother; now the memory of Laura and any legacy of her possessions were worthless to Chrissie. She wanted nothing from that self-centered woman's life to stain the simplicity of her own. This man was here to force the intrusion of Laura's reality, Laura's affairs, into her life. She just knew it. There could be no other possible explanation for a visit by an attorney who'd traveled all the way from California to see her.

Chrissie's first instinct was to slam the door in the man's face, to shut out whatever he'd come here to say to her. But she couldn't do it. It would only be postponing the inevitable. She supposed she wouldn't be able to avoid it forever.

Besides, the poor guy was wet, shivering and, at the moment, possibly a great deal more unhappy than she was about his being here. Ordinary human compassion compelled Chrissie to offer the man a brief respite from the storm while he said his piece.

She stepped back so that he could enter. As she closed the door, she pointed toward the hallway. "The bathroom's that way, on the left. There are plenty of towels on the racks. I'll put on some coffee."

"Thanks." Andrew Casey's voice was deep, pleasant and filled with unmistakable gratitude. He followed her directions while Chrissie went the opposite way toward her small kitchen.

With automatic, practiced motions, she put coffee on to brew. The rich sauce she'd left simmering on the range when Jim called was sending out an enticing aroma. Chrissie lifted the lid, stirred and turned down the heat. Funny, she thought, how quickly her appetite had fled the moment the man had introduced himself.

The subject of her thoughts entered the room. Andrew Casey had towel-dried his hair and combed it so that it lay in neat order above a high, broad brow. His gray slacks were almost black with dampness, and he'd removed the coat.

His pale blue dress shirt was damp, as well, and it clung snugly to his lean torso and well-shaped shoulders. There was something almost blatantly sensual about the way the cloth starkly outlined his chest. Fleetingly Chrissie thought that she might have admired the man's obvious physical charms if he'd been anyone other than who he was. Resolutely she raised her gaze to his face. It was safer and more sensible.

"Something in here smells out-of-this-world! You must be a fantastic cook." Andrew Casey favored her with a winsome smile.

Chrissie rather liked the open, friendly smile, and she found herself returning it before she shrugged. "In New Orleans it's a matter of pride to be an accomplished cook."

"So I've heard. What are you making, if you don't mind my asking?"

"Shrimp Creole. Ever tasted it?"

"Can't say that I have. My mother is more of a meat-and-potatoes type of cook. As for me, I'm the sort who scorches water. I never go near my stove except to heat a frozen dinner occasionally."

Chrissie laughed and said in a consoling tone, "I'm sure you have other talents instead."

"Except for football, which is in the distant past, I can't think of any offhand." A faint embarrassment quirked Drew's lips as he changed the subject. "Considering you don't know anything about me, it was awfully decent of you to let me in to make use of your bathroom. Thanks a lot."

"Well, I have a rule against allowing people to drip all over the living room carpet. Besides, I already know everything about you that I need to know." She took two coffee mugs from a cupboard.

"You do?" His eyebrows rose in a quizzical expression.

"Sure." Chrissie poured coffee into the mugs and said calmly, "You're here about *her*. Laura Douglas."

Andrew Casey looked taken aback. "You know?"

Chrissie handed his coffee to him, then picked up her own mug and led the way into the living room. "That she was my birth mother, yes." Her voice remained steady and emotionless. "You're probably here to tell me I'm in her will."

"Do you have a crystal ball or something? It was my understanding that you didn't know about Miss Douglas... that she was your mother, I mean."

They sat down on opposite ends of the sofa. Drew supposed he should have been prepared to meet a vision of beauty, considering Christina Barrows was Laura Douglas's daughter, but he hadn't given it a thought before he saw her. Her hair, more golden than Laura's had been, billowed charmingly around her face. There was no trace of makeup on her flawless skin, and yet it glowed with beauty. She was dressed in a pair of blue shorts and a pink T-shirt, and she didn't seem to be at all aware of just how sexy she looked. Drew was used to beautiful women—L.A. teemed with them—but this one outshone them all in his estimation.

She shook her head in response to his question. "No crystal balls or psychic powers. My parents... my adoptive parents...told me the day she died. They said something like this...your visit...might be possible. Mr. Casey..." Chrissie paused and inhaled. "You've made this trip for nothing. I don't want anything that belonged to Laura Douglas."

It was a nice-sounding, high-minded little speech, but Drew didn't buy it for one minute. And anyway, whether she meant it or not was immaterial. He'd been given a job to do, and he intended to do it. Besides, there was something important he had to tell her, something she couldn't possibly know.

"Look, Miss Barrows, I've had a long day. My plane was an hour and a half late. It was pouring buckets when I arrived. And although I waited until the worst of the storm let up before leaving the hotel to come find you, the heavens opened up again, and I had a near accident on the way over here. I got lost trying to find your street, and just to make my day complete, I got drenched running from the car up to your balcony. I'm tired, I'm wet and cold, and hungry. I appreciate the loan of your bath towels and for the hot coffee, but I'd appreciate it even more if you'd at least listen to what I was sent here to tell you. If I fail in my assignment, I'll probably get fired. And then I'll be thrown out of my apartment and I'll become a homeless bum wandering the streets, and it'll be your fault. Now you really don't want to be responsible for that, do you?"

"If you got fired, you could always try script writing for the movies," Chrissie said dryly. "That's quite a vivid scenario."

Drew grinned. "You'll hear me out, then?"

Chrissie gazed at him consideringly for a long moment. Finally she reached a decision. "Tell you what . . . I'll listen to what you have to say later. Meanwhile you're in New Orleans, Mr. Casey, and you just admitted you're hungry. How would you like to try some authentic Creole food?"

Drew's grin broadened. "Miss Barrows...I thought you'd never ask."

Chapter Two

I'm sorry I don't have any wine to offer you with dinner."

"Don't be. I need a clear head to drive back to the hotel through all that rain, anyway."

"Good point." Chrissie paused with her hand on the refrigerator door and turned to grin mischievously at Drew. "As a conversational topic, I'd ask you what you think of New Orleans, but I'm afraid you might tell me."

Drew grinned back. "Not too favorable tonight," he admitted. "But I came for Mardi Gras a few years ago and had a great time. This town sure knows how to throw a party."

"Of course. Our city founders invented *les bon temps*." Chrissie's head disappeared behind the open refrigerator door, reemerging a moment later as she balanced in her hands a head of lettuce, a couple of tomatoes and a carrot.

Drew, with his shoulder supported against the kitchen door frame, watched her in silent admiration. She was of medium height—he'd noticed earlier that the top of her head reached his shoulder—and she was slender and shapely. Very shapely. His gaze was drawn from her back downward, taking note of the interesting indication of a small waist hidden beneath the T-shirt, and below that, a well-rounded behind covered by the blue shorts. Her bare legs were long and lovely, a soft peach gold. Even her sandaled feet were nice, small and dainty with pale pink manicured toenails. In a simpler, more natural fashion, she was as beautiful as her famous mother had been.

Yet Drew could detect only faint traces of any resemblance between mother and daughter. Chrissie's hair was more blond than red, and her eyes were a lustrous deep blue instead of the doe brown Laura's had been. Her features were more softly defined than Laura's, too, and in Drew's opinion, far more appealing. Laura Douglas's beauty had been the dramatic sort—fiery, compelling, exotic. On screen she'd been the epitome of the classic femme fatale, the seductress, the fantasy of every man who in reality would be uneasy with such a woman. Chrissie's beauty was a gentler sort, the kind that appealed to a man's notions of chivalry and honorable intent rather than inspiring great obsessions. Her beauty was more approachable and, in the long run, the type most men ultimately sought when choosing a mate.

That realization brought fresh bitterness to Drew. That had been his problem with Carol. He'd been a blind sucker and had fallen for glamour instead of character. He'd known all along that Carol was different from the sort of women his mother and two sisters-in-law were, but he'd kidded himself into believing it would work out anyway.

Not that Laura Douglas's on-screen image had had any bearing on reality, he reminded himself. Her long-term marriage to Martin Timms had never produced a breath of scandal within scandal-ridden Hollywood. By the same token, just because Chrissie appeared to be clean-cut and unpretentious, who knew what she was really like underneath?

Drew had learned his lesson when it came to making snap judgments about women.

Anyway, it didn't really matter to him what Chrissie was like as a person. She was only a professional case to him. All the same he couldn't deny that he'd been immensely pleased when she'd invited him to dinner. He hadn't been looking forward to a solitary meal.

"Can I help with anything?" he asked.

The knife she'd been slicing tomatoes with halted in mid-air as Chrissie turned from the counter and gazed at him. Her eyebrows rose and the blue eyes sparkled. "That from a man who tells me he scorches water?"

Drew grinned. "I felt duty-bound to make the offer anyway. If I'd had any idea I'd be invited to dinner, I'd have brought you flowers or candy or something."

Chrissie shrugged, turned back to the cutting board and said, "It's no big deal. There's plenty of food."

"Do you always make mouth-watering meals like this one just for yourself?" he asked in amazement.

"No. But I enjoy cooking, and now that school is out, I have the time to indulge myself."

"School?"

"I'm a teacher."

"That so? What grade?" Drew left the doorway, walked over to stand beside her, snitched a tomato wedge and popped it into his mouth.

"Third."

"My third-grade teacher was Mrs. Waggoner. She had dark beetle eyes, another pair in the back of her head, a double chin that wavered every time she spoke and—when she was riled—a booming voice that would transport you to the next county. They sure didn't make teachers like you in my day!"

"Oh, I don't know. I may not have the double chin or the dark beetle eyes, but I, too, have a second pair of eyes in the back of my head. It's a requirement for earning your teacher's accreditation. And believe me, when I'm angry, my students are left in no doubt about it.''

"Umm, if you say so," Drew said dubiously. "I'll betcha all the little boys in the class are in love with you."

Chrissie grinned and admitted, "I've had a couple of suitors among them. One boy wanted to give me his pet worm as a token of his affection."

"Ah, the eternal symbol of love." Drew chuckled, then asked curiously, "Speaking of suitors, does an older version exist?"

"No one in particular," Chrissie replied easily. "What about you? Are you married or involved in a relationship?"

"Nope." The subject had suited him fine as long as it had focused on Chrissie, but Drew had no desire to discuss his own shattered love life, so he said, "If you'll tell me where you keep the dishes and silverware, I'll set the table. I'm not as bad at breaking things as I am at burning food."

Chrissie pointed to a cupboard. "Plates and glasses there, silverware in the second drawer on the right."

While Drew set the table, Chrissie filled a serving bowl with the savory entrée and took a loaf of garlic-buttered French bread from the oven. She had to admit to herself that for a man she hadn't wanted to let in the door, Drew was okay. He was likable, pleasant company for a rainy evening, and so far at least she didn't regret her impulsive invitation. As long as she could forget why he had really come, she could enjoy his being there.

She had to admit, too, that it was rather nice to have a congenial male visitor. It could hardly be compared to an actual date, since they'd known each other less than an hour, but it was still definitely nice. She couldn't remember the last time she'd had a man to dinner—probably two or three months ago—so it made an exciting change.

And anyway, this was actually better. Tonight there would be no tension over unwanted romantic pressures; they were simply two people spending an evening together, and they could get acquainted without such bothersome considerations getting in the way.

Chrissie was a little weary of the romantic scene. She hadn't met any man she'd really liked in a long time . . . not since Barry, and it had been two years since they'd broken up. None of the first dates she'd had during the past six or eight months had evolved into second ones because she'd realized it would only have been a waste of time. And yet she was young and single, and she often got lonely from spending too many evenings alone.

Dinner was a success. Drew raved about the meal. Chrissie was pleased to realize his praises were genuine, because he helped himself to seconds of everything.

"How come you're not married?" he asked teasingly. "You cook like an angel."

Chrissie laughed. "I didn't know angels cooked."

"Well, if they did, they'd cook like this," Drew declared. He sighed and put down his fork at last.

"There's a little bit of the Shrimp Creole left," Chrissie pointed out. "Why don't you finish it off, Drew?"

They'd gotten on a first-name basis during the meal.

Drew shook his head, and his voice was filled with regret. "I wish I could, I truly do, but I just don't have any place to put it. Thanks for inviting me, Chrissie. This meal has more than made up for the day I've had."

Chrissie felt her face warming beneath his glowing words and intense gaze, and then she felt silly. Imagine actually feeling a shy, deep pleasure over a stranger's compliments! Besides, women of the eighties had far more important things to be respected for than their culinary abilities!

Severely admonishing herself, she got to her feet and said briskly, "I'm glad you liked it. I'll just clear the table and bring in more coffee, and then we can get down to business."

Drew felt a slight letdown. Not that he objected to doing the job he came for—but until now, he'd been able to put business considerations into the back of his mind and simply enjoy himself. It had been a pleasure talking with Chrissie. She'd been open and friendly, and conversation had been easy. He'd especially liked her ability to poke fun at herself and life in general. He'd liked her smile, too. When she smiled, her eyes glowed like blue fire and an endearing dimple peeped out on the left side of her mouth. Altogether it had been a wonderful, cosy evening.

While Chrissie was in the kitchen, Drew left the dining table and walked into the living room. He gazed about at the numerous potted plants that thrived in the room. The kitchen and bathroom were enlivened with greenery, too. The plants gave a bright, cheerful effect, lifting the room above what was otherwise an ordinary, unremarkable apartment. The simple yet eloquent touches seemed to speak clearly of the character of the apartment's occupant, of a woman who loved the beauty of nature, who loved the real things of life, earthy things, the important things. He wondered almost sadly how much her inheritance would change that character.

Chrissie rejoined him with their coffee, and this time while Drew sat on the sofa and spread out papers from his briefcase, she took a nearby chair.

She frowned as she eyed the thick sheaf of papers. "Is that a copy of—" The words were like cotton in her mouth. "—Laura's will?"

"Yes. It's quite detailed, but—"

Chrissie interrupted. "If you expect me to sit up all night reading it, think again. Just tell me the part that I have to know."

Drew sighed and leaned back against the sofa as he gave her a direct gaze. "The thing is, that's practically everything. I'll be leaving you this copy so you can look it over when you have time, but if you want it summed up in a nutshell, you've inherited one-half of her entire estate. I can't give you an exact figure, because the accountants are still working on it and it's going to take some time to get a bottom-line figure, but it's safe to say it'll come to several million."

"S-several?" Chrissie was so startled she could scarcely speak.

Drew nodded. "Of course that's not all in liquid cash, you understand. There's the house in Bel Air, investment properties, stocks and bonds, and also jewelry. You are now quite a wealthy young woman, Chrissie."

She gave her head a small shake. "I don't...I don't want it."

Drew ignored the statement. "Laura designated you to be the sole executor of the estate, but with a qualifier. You have the full power to buy or sell anything belonging to the estate, but one-half of any money you may receive from selling something such as the house must go into a trust fund for the other heir."

"I don't understand. Who inherits the other half? And why must it go into a trust?"

Drew leaned forward and, surprising her, took one of her hands in his. "Hang on to your hat, Chrissie. I'm about to give you a big shock."

Chrissie laughed nervously. "I doubt it. I'm numb from the shocks I've already received...learning who my mother was, that she left me a...a fortune." Her voice trembled slightly. "What else could you possibly have to tell me that would top that?"

"You have an identical twin sister."

She'd been wrong. He did manage to shock her after all. Chrissie felt as though someone had just slammed a fist into her midsection. She stopped breathing, and her eyes glazed as she stared at him in disbelief.

After an endless moment, her breathing resumed with a ragged gasping intake of air. Chrissie's skin went cold then hot, and all at once she was shaking violently while her heart thudded like thunder. When she was finally able to form words once more and push them from her constricted throat, she whispered, "Are you *sure*? Can that possibly be true?"

"Laura left a letter of explanation with instructions that it be opened by her attorneys at the time of her death."

"A sister. A *twin* sister." Chrissie whispered the words to herself, trying to absorb their meaning. Yet the words floated through her mind, wispy, insubstantial, a concept she was unable to grasp. Learning the true identity of her mother faded in pale comparison. She'd always known her mother was out there somewhere, a blank face, to be sure, but there'd been the knowledge that such a person existed. But a sister? Her very own identical twin—someone who must be a mirror of herself? It was too much, too stunning to even dream, much less to comprehend or believe.

Hope struggled inside her, but Chrissie was afraid of such feelings and she blocked them out. Maybe Drew was wrong. Maybe Laura had never written such a letter. Maybe someone else had as a cruel, cruel joke. Or maybe Laura had done it herself as a means of hurting Chrissie yet a second time—the first time by giving her away; the second, by giving her a false hope.

And yet that was farfetched in the extreme. Laura had left her, Chrissie, one-half of her estate, a considerable fortune, so why would she have wanted to perpetrate such a horrible hoax against her own daughter? Therefore it really must be true!

She searched Drew's face, his dark eyes, for the slightest evidence of lying, but all she saw was sincerity. His gaze was steady and unwavering, and his expression was one of concern while she dealt with the emotional impact of his astonishing news.

Chrissie's eyes were suddenly swimming with shimmering tears—tears of hope that blossomed after all, that expanded and caressed her entire being with tender rose-velvet petals of growing joy. She was unconscious of the hand still in Drew's, of her fingers curling tighter around his as she clung to him for strength. "Tell me," she begged huskily. "Tell me everything."

"When she was eighteen, Laura was working as a fashion model when she got the chance to go to London on an assignment. While she was there, she required surgery because of an acute appendix. There were complications, and a long recuperation period followed. The hospital staff arranged for her to recuperate in a private home, in the care of a retired nurse.

"While she was there, the nurse's nephew came to visit. He was almost twenty years older than Laura, an intellectual man who wrote in-depth historical texts. He and Laura were married a short time later, and that man was your father."

"My parents were actually married, then?" Chrissie asked in wonder. "Naturally I always thought...always assumed..."

Drew cleared his throat. "Yes...well...you were legitimate, all right. But the marriage didn't last. Not too surprising, perhaps, given the enormous differences in their backgrounds, personalities and ages. Anyway, according to Laura's letter, even before the twins were born, she and Nigel were having difficulties."

"Nigel?" Chrissie hastily brushed away the tears that glistened in her eyes, and her voice was eager. "You know my father's name, then?"

"It's Nigel Littleton. But..." Drew's voice dropped a notch. "He's deceased, too, Chrissie. We checked the L.A. library, and they actually have a couple of his books there, so we were able to get the name of his publishing house in London. They told us he died three years ago."

Chrissie nodded and stared stonily at a shelf on the window that was lined with African violets. What good did it do, learning the identities of both her parents now when they were gone? All that it brought was an aching emptiness.

"Go on," she said dully. "My sister... you haven't told me about her yet."

Drew picked up Chrissie's untouched coffee from the tray on the low table in front of the sofa. "Here. Drink this. You look a little pale."

Mechanically Chrissie accepted the cup, took a sip, then nodded. "I'm fine. Go on."

"Right. Nigel and Laura separated and divorced almost immediately after your birth. But they made an agreement that each of them would keep one of the twins. Your father got custody of your sister, Victoria; Laura got you. You were around three months old at the time." Drew paused and glanced down at the will, not because he needed to look at it, but because he couldn't bear the glimmer of hope on Chrissie's face. "They agreed that neither of them would ever try to see or communicate with the other twin, the one given up, and that they would never tell you girls that you actually had a twin."

"Why?" Chrissie cried out in protest. "Why would they deliberately be so cruel as to cheat us of that knowledge?"

Drew shook his head, still avoiding her eyes. "Laura didn't explain their reasons in her letter," he said gently. "All I can figure is that they did it to protect themselves from each other...from loneliness. Because Laura brought you back with her to the United States and that left an ocean between them. Maybe they were afraid that if they shared you, allowing intercontinental visits, one of them would be tricked into losing custody. Or maybe they thought that if you girls knew about each other, you'd plead to be allowed to grow up together, in which case that would have pressured one parent to be without a child.''

''But Laura didn't want me, anyway!'' Chrissie was stricken with an overwhelming bitterness. ''Don't misunderstand me...I love my adoptive parents with all my heart. I've been given a wonderful life of love and security with them, and I can never regret being raised by them. They *are* my real parents in every way. But tell me why Laura brought me to this country with her if she didn't want to keep me? Why didn't she leave me there with my father and my sister? Or send me back when she chose to give me up?'' She almost choked over the words as she thought of the magnitude of all she'd been denied.

Drew spread his hands. ''I don't have any answers. Maybe she hated your father—I just don't know. At dinner you told me your adoptive parents had met her and that they'd exchanged letters all these years. Maybe Laura felt that by placing you with a couple in this country, a couple who was also willing to give her news of you, she could remain closer to you than if she sent you back to England. The only thing she said about that in the letter is that at the time she gave you up, she was broke and couldn't support you.''

''I was eight months old! Eight months old, and she decided life was a little tough, so she gave me away to someone else instead of returning me to my own flesh-and-blood relatives! She denied me any chance to know my own father, to grow up with a twin sister! I...I think I'll always despise her for that!''

"Hey!" Drew exclaimed softly. "Anger won't get you anywhere. I know you feel—"

"What would you know of my feelings?" Chrissie snapped harshly. "Were you ever given up for adoption by one of the wealthiest, most beautiful, most celebrated and apparently most selfish and vindictive women in the world?"

"Well, no, but she wasn't wealthy when—"

"Were you ever denied any knowledge of having a twin, an *identical* twin who shares this same planet, just because two people were possessive and self-centered? God, how my parents must have hated each other to do that to their own children!"

"Look, I know this is all quite a blow to you," Drew said, "but try to look on the bright side of this."

"What bright side, may I ask, and if you say Laura's money, I swear I'll throw something at you!"

Drew grinned. In a way Chrissie's anger was good. It flooded her cheeks with blood and sizzled in her fiery gaze, displacing that earlier stunned numbness that had paralyzed her.

"Not the money," he replied. "I mean that in the end, Laura came through for you. She honored her agreement with your father until both of them were gone, but then she broke her silence and left that letter. Don't you see...it's her gift to you...the information that you have a twin in existence."

Chrissie was somewhat mollified. Drew was right. Knowing that was an incredible, spectacular gift. "You said her name is Victoria," she said in a milder tone. "Where is she?"

Drew got to his feet and walked to the window. The rain still splashed against the windowpanes, but with far less intensity now.

"What is it?" He hadn't realized Chrissie had followed him until she spoke just behind him. Her voice shook. "What's wrong? You're not . . . you're not going to tell me that she . . . that she's dead, too, are you? Please . . . not that!"

Drew turned quickly and put his hands on her shoulders. Now that they stood so close, he caught a faint scent of perfume . . . something floral like a summer flower garden. And she *did* just reach his shoulder in height. Her head was tilted back as she looked up at him, and her eyes were dark with anxiety. Her pink lips quivered. Drew wondered at his sudden yearning to kiss her.

He refrained from following up on that impulse. Her gaze was troubled, and it was important for him to banish that fear as quickly as he could. "As far as I know, Victoria's alive and healthy. It's just that we don't know where she is. I've already launched a search, but . . ." He left the obvious uncertainty of the outcome unstated.

Chrissie's shoulders drooped. All her spirit seemed to be draining out of her. She realized she was tired, emotionally exhausted. She'd been on an emotional seesaw all week, and now this . . . the final blow. She had a sister, a twin, who might be anywhere.

"Listen to me, Chrissie," Drew said with as much vigor as he could muster. "I promise you I'm going to do everything in my power to locate her."

"I wish you hadn't told me," she responded wearily. "Why even tell me if you can't lead me to her? In its own way, that's as cruel as my parents keeping the knowledge of each other's existence from my sister and me in the first place."

"I had to tell you," Drew said softly. "You had to know because of the inheritance."

"Oh, that." Chrissie waved a hand of dismissal and turned away from him. "I told you to begin with that I don't want anything that belonged to Laura. I meant that. I don't need her money!'' She buried her face in her hands, close to tears again, close to sobbing. She swallowed painfully and fought to regain control.

Drew spoke from behind her. "I'm sorry. But whether you want it or not, it's yours. It's your responsibility now. There are legal matters only you can take care of—papers to sign, decisions to make. The whole obligation is on your shoulders until your sister has been found.''

Chrissie sighed and turned toward Drew. "And what happens if you don't find her?'' she asked dully.

"Laura put a time limit of five years on Victoria's trust fund. Our law firm has been instructed to aggressively attempt to locate her during that period of time, but if we haven't been able to do so when the five years are up, the entire estate will belong to you.''

"No!''

"Yes.'' Drew's voice was firm and compelling. "We'll find Victoria if it's at all possible. I give you my word I won't leave any stone unturned, any lead unchecked. But in the meantime, you must come to California immediately and assume control of Laura Douglas's estate . . . for your sister's welfare, as well as for your own.''

Chapter Three

Clattering food trays, murmuring voices, the scrape of chairs, the shuffling of footsteps all blended into a dull roar. It was dimly perceived and subconsciously ignored by most of the patrons who occupied tables in the airport coffee shop. To Christina, the ordinary noises seemed extraordinarily loud; they pounded into her head like the jarring, vibrating racket of a jackhammer.

She was sitting at a corner table with her parents, killing time by having a cup of coffee while they waited for her flight to be called. Chrissie opened her purse and began poking around inside it.

"What're you looking for?" her mother asked.

"Aspirin. I'm getting a headache." Chrissie found the tiny box, took two tablets from it and popped them into her mouth.

"It's not like you to be so nervous. You're letting this business get to you too much," her father observed.

Chrissie smiled wanly. "Who me, nervous? Now why would I be nervous just because I've got a few million reasons?"

Jack Barrows laughed. "There're lots of people in the world who would love to have your problem."

"Then let them take my place," Chrissie snapped. "I didn't ask for the job. I don't want Laura's money or her problems. I liked my life just the way it was."

It had been five days since Drew Casey had arrived on her doorstep, five days during which she'd had ample time for her emotions to work her into a state of high anxiety. In a few more minutes she would board a plane for Los Angeles, and she'd never dreaded anything more in her entire life. She felt as though a huge boulder had come down to rest on her narrow shoulders, the weight of an unwanted and frightening responsibility for which she was entirely unqualified.

"It is a little overwhelming," Marie conceded, "suddenly having all that money and the responsibility that comes with it. But you'll do just fine, *chérie*. You're smart and you've always been levelheaded."

Chrissie sighed, and her voice was wistful. "I still wish you were coming with me. I could use the moral support. Or better yet, I wish I could forget all this and go with you tomorrow to Colorado. Right now a relaxing vacation in the Rockies sounds awfully good to me."

"You know we love you and would do almost anything for you." Her mother's voice was gentle. "But your father and I both agree that you'll do better without our influence. You've had a lot of shocks lately and you haven't had time to deal with them yet, to face up to them."

"We're still your parents, Chrissie," Jack said solemnly. "Nothing will change that. But now you know the truth about your background, and that's a part of your life, too...a part that's separate from us. Like it or not, it's a part of you, too, and you have to learn to accept it and make your peace with it. Right now you resent the money because you resent Laura. Maybe you've got a good reason for feeling that way, but you've got to find a way to get past your bitterness toward her or you're never going to be happy.''

"I don't know if I can get past it, Dad,'' Chrissie replied. "Anyway, my problem is more than resentment. What do I know about investment properties, stocks and bonds and the like? I'm going to have to make decisions about those things, but what if I make the wrong choices? If I mess up, I could lose a fortune, not just my share, but my sister's, too. I'm plain scared of being responsible for somebody else's money.''

"Just don't do anything in haste,'' her father advised. "Learn all you can, ask for advice from the experts, and then after you've weighed everything, do the best you can. You're smart. You won't go far wrong.''

"I wish I had your faith,'' Chrissie said unsteadily. The announcement that her flight was boarding came over the loudspeaker. "I guess this is it.'' She sighed, getting to her feet.

Her parents embraced her. Marie whispered, "I hope so much they'll have located Victoria by the time you get there.''

"Me, too,'' Chrissie answered fervently. "Oh, me, too!''

"You've got the phone numbers I gave you?'' she asked her father as he wrapped his arms around her.

"Yep. Laura's home number, the hotel and the law firm. We'll call you as soon as we get settled in a hotel in Colorado. By then you'll have had a few days to get the lay of the land. Good luck, honey.''

Chrissie went toward her boarding gate and got in line, and while she stood there, she realized she'd never felt so alone in her life. It was as though everything familiar and safe had abruptly been stripped away. She no longer had a support system. Wobbly legs or not, the time had come to stand on her own two feet without the loving, ever-ready assistance of her parents.

Outwardly she'd been on her own since her college days. She'd spent four years in Baton Rouge at school, returning home only for holidays and occasional weekends. After graduation she'd returned to New Orleans to teach, but she had taken an apartment of her own. Supposedly she was an independent adult, making her own decisions, living her own life free from parental authority, interference or advice. All that was well and good, but now she realized that in reality she'd never stopped leaning on her mother and father. Financially she'd supported herself, of course, and she was proud of that, but emotionally...well, her folks had simply always been there for her whenever she'd needed them.

Now it was time to step forward on her own, and she understood her parents' decision not to accompany her to California. Nothing could ever alter the truth that they were her real parents; nothing could ever snap the close bond between them. But settling Laura Douglas's estate was her affair, not theirs. There was no logical reason for them to get involved. And dealing with all the emotions that boiled inside her about Laura was something that only she could do. It was beyond her parents' ability to help, and they'd been smart enough to see that before she did.

The line began to move forward briskly, and a few minutes later Chrissie was in her window seat on the plane, idly watching as other passengers milled in the narrow aisles, shoving belongings into the overhead compartments.

A rather large man came to take the seat next to her, and Chrissie abruptly felt wedged into a tiny prison. As she nodded companionably, she realized in a flash that she needn't have flown coach. She could have afforded a roomier, more comfortable seat in the first-class section.

She almost laughed out loud at the strange notion. Her traveling had always been of the bare-bones budget variety, and until this very instant, it hadn't occurred to her that this trip might be any different. The irony of it amused her. Being rich, she decided, was going to take some getting used to. Maybe there ought to be a course for it in universities—How To Act Wealthy 101.

It was a dark flash of humor and gone almost at once. No matter how much money Laura Douglas had left to her, it could never make up for having robbed her of her own twin sister all her life; stolen from her, too, a father who probably would've been more than happy to have raised her, as well as Victoria. And even later, after Chrissie had been adopted, Laura could have at any time let her know she had a twin. By then there would've been no question but that Chrissie would want to remain with the only parents she'd ever known, but at least she could've been aware she had an identical twin sister. She might have been able to contact her, to exchange letters and maybe even a visit. All the millions Laura was supposed to have willed to her could never buy Chrissie's forgiveness for cheating her of that.

Besides the headaches that the responsibility of all the money was already giving her, Chrissie couldn't imagine what she might do with it. Beyond her desire to buy a new car to replace her old secondhand Buick, she couldn't think of a single thing she wanted that she couldn't already afford. Heaven knows a schoolteacher doesn't get rich off her salary, but Chrissie didn't exactly feel poor or deprived, either. She earned enough to live on—modestly, perhaps—but enough. She had never been hung up on the idea of having lots of money or showy possessions.

Neither had her parents. Jack Barrows owned and operated a small dry cleaning business, and while it had never made them wealthy, he and Marie were quite comfortable and content with their life the way it was. The Barrows home was an ordinary frame house, old-fashioned but roomy. Her parents' car was a late-model one, and there were savings in the bank for their retirement years ahead. Jack had always maintained that as long as he could provide a roof over their heads, clothes on their backs and food on the table, anything else was gravy. Actually they had the gravy, too, in the form of yearly vacation trips and a few other luxuries from time to time. Chrissie could think of nothing she might be able to buy for them that they would really want, much less actually need.

No, she concluded, Laura Douglas's legacy was nothing more than a bother. All Chrissie really wanted was to find her twin sister.

Every time she thought of Victoria, a strange feeling came over her. She tried hard to visualize someone who looked just like her—a living, breathing, exact physical replica of herself. It was impossible.

Yet fiercely, passionately she ached with the desire to meet Victoria. She wanted to look into her eyes, to see her face, to touch her. She wanted to be able to bridge the empty gap of years and connect their lives by a bond that transcended those lost years. Chrissie wasn't sure that would ever be possible, though, even if they were to meet today. Sisters they might be, identical twins they might be—but the fact remained that they'd grown up separately, in different countries, in different cultures. Their values, beliefs, hopes and dreams might be so far apart that there would be little room for belated sisterly closeness.

But for now, such questions were so much wasted thought. Victoria hadn't been located, at least not as of yesterday. Drew Casey had returned to Los Angeles the day after he'd visited Chrissie at her apartment, but they'd been in touch several times by phone. Yesterday he'd called to let her know what hotel he'd booked her into and to confirm the arrival time of her flight, and he'd told her he hadn't made any progress in trying to find her sister.

The plane lifted into the air, and Chrissie's neighbor in the next seat took some business papers from his briefcase. She was glad he didn't want to talk, because her headache had turned worse. She leaned back against her seat, closed her eyes and tried to blank out everything . . . her thoughts, her fellow passengers, the throbbing hum of the plane itself.

By a small miracle, she actually managed to fall asleep. When she awakened over an hour later, she felt enormously better. The dreadful headache was gone at last.

In the tiny restroom compartment, Chrissie dashed her face with water, combed her hair and applied fresh lipstick, and that, too, did much to restore her equilibrium.

Lunch was being served by the stewardesses by the time she returned to her seat, and she even managed to eat some of it. She exchanged brief, cordial chitchat with her neighbor in the next seat during the meal, and it made a pleasant change.

She wasn't sorry, though, when afterward the man went back to his work. Relieved from the obligation of making further small talk, Chrissie gazed out the window at the landscape below and wondered how long the estate business matters would keep her in Los Angeles. Fortunately it was summer and school was out. She could stay for several weeks if need be.

She had never been to California, though she'd always wanted to visit there someday. Now, however, she could whip up no zest for the prospect. Little had she dreamed that this was the type of visit she would eventually make. Life was certainly surprising sometimes.

Chrissie sighed and glanced at her watch. Thirty minutes now. Thirty more minutes and the plane would be landing.

When he'd called, Drew had promised to meet her plane this afternoon. Chrissie was grateful for his thoughtfulness. Knowing she would see him again was the only bright spot in an otherwise thoroughly depressing journey.

She had genuinely liked Drew. He'd been witty and fun and unexpectedly easy to talk with, considering they'd only just met. His presence had turned a dismal rainy evening into something extraordinary, something special, at least until they'd had to settle down and discuss the business he'd come to see her about. It would be good to have a kind, familiar face among all the strange ones she would be encountering during her stay in L.A.; it was comforting to feel she had made a friend, that she had someone she could turn to.

From his position, Drew had a good view of the passengers leaving the plane. As he watched for Chrissie, he was a little surprised at how eagerly he anticipated seeing her again.

He'd practically broken his neck to get here on time. A meeting at the office had run on longer than he'd expected, making him late. Then when he'd arrived at the airport, there'd been the inevitable frustration of searching for a parking spot. After he'd finally found one, he'd loped toward the terminal, unhappily convinced that after all his efforts, he'd missed her. People always complained about late planes; he did it himself without compunction. But this was one time he was relieved to be greeted by the news of a delay.

A stout man came along the ramp and into the lounge and finally, there just behind him, Drew saw her. That night in New Orleans, she'd been wearing shorts and a T-shirt and no makeup. She'd been beautiful then; now she was spectacular. Before stepping forward to meet her, he stood still for a moment, just enjoying the sight of her. Today Chrissie wore a khaki dress trimmed with crimson. It was tailored and the coloring went well with her fiery-gold hair and rich creamy skin. Her lips were a soft raspberry red, giving her face exactly the brightness it needed to offset the red trim on the dress. She looked dazzling.

She reached the lounge and began looking from right to left as she searched for him. Drew moved forward, zigging and zagging around several other people blocking his path, until he could finally reach her.

"Hi. Remember me?"

Drew slipped the strap of Chrissie's carry-on bag from her shoulder and swung it easily over his own.

She favored him with a smile that, to Drew, seemed to outshine the fabled California sunshine.

"Hi, yourself," she said. "I'm sorry the plane was so late. Have you been waiting long?"

"Actually," he admitted, "I barely made it on time. I got stuck in a meeting and I was afraid I'd missed you altogether."

"I'm glad you didn't," Chrissie said fervently.

"Not as glad as I am," Drew answered with a smile. He pointed a finger, saying, "That way to baggage claim."

As they walked, they talked little because it was so difficult. Crowds swelled and thinned around them, only to swell again.

At last they collected Chrissie's luggage and made their way to Drew's car, and shortly afterward they were speeding along the freeway.

"Welcome to L.A.," Drew said in the deliberately cheerful manner of a tour guide. "Observe now, if you will, our remarkable system of traffic congestion, guaranteed to frustrate even a saint. It took many years of painstaking effort for us to evolve a plan that would provide maximum stress on the nerves and patience of drivers. Overhead you'll note faint traces of our renowned smog, although unfortunately today it isn't quite so visible as it is on our finest, most oppressive days. However, if you extend your visit for at least several days, you're bound to have a wonderful view of it soon, unimpeded by clear blue skies and bright sunlight."

Chrissie chuckled. "I must say you make a strong sales pitch for your hometown. You've almost convinced me to forsake all those nice rainstorms, mosquitoes, humidity and occasional hurricanes we have in New Orleans and move out here."

"If I were you, I'd seriously consider it." Drew grinned, then turned serious. "Until I saw you, I wasn't entirely certain you would really come."

"I didn't want to, believe me." Chrissie sighed heavily. "But my parents convinced me that I had to do this. Have you had any word of Victoria?"

Drew heard the rising hope in her voice and he hated to have to disappoint her again, but there was no way around it. He kept his eyes on the road, but he shook his head and answered, "Not yet, but these things take a while, Chrissie. I put a man in London onto it even before I visited you in New Orleans. He's an attorney with a firm there that we do business with from time to time. Bill Chamberlain is very reliable, and he'll do everything he can to find her. He's already checking out the last known address your father's publishers had listed, and then he'll go from there. If we get lucky, we might hear something quite soon, but then again it could take a long, long time. You've got to be prepared for that, you know. Victoria could be anywhere in the whole wide world."

"That's what worries me," Chrissie said softly. "It's just that I want so badly to find her that..." Her voice broke, and she sighed and fell silent.

Drew glanced at her briefly before eyeing the traffic again. His voice was gentle. "I understand. Hey," he added encouragingly, ''some news...a solid lead or something is bound to turn up before too long.''

''You think so?''

''Sure.''

He didn't know whether he believed it or not, but he'd had to say it. Drew knew if he'd just learned he had a long-lost sister, he'd be half-crazy with impatience until he found her, and he already had two brothers. How much more urgently must Chrissie desire it when her sister was the only blood relative she had in the world?

As though by sheer determination, Chrissie changed the subject, and her voice became crisp. ''Okay, give me the agenda. What do I have to do first now that I'm here?''

''Tomorrow morning we'll have a conference meeting at the office. You get off easy today. I'm going to drop you off at your hotel, give you a couple of hours to catch your breath, and then I'll return for you and we'll have dinner together. I want to repay you for that great meal you served me. All right with you?''

Chrissie gave him a look of mock horror. ''You're not planning to cook for me, are you?''

''And serve scorched water?'' Drew's eyes twinkled. ''Well, I considered it, but I finally decided it might be too heavy a meal for you. No...you'll just have to settle for a restaurant. What are your views on Chinese food?''

''Fairly high as long as I don't have to get on another plane and go to China for it.''

They exchanged bad jokes until they reached the hotel. After registering, Chrissie parted from Drew in the lobby and followed the bellhop toward the elevator.

In spite of her nap on the plane, she hadn't slept well for nearly two weeks—ever since learning Laura Douglas was her mother—and the fatigue was speedily sapping her energy. She was tired, stiff from being cramped in the tight seat on the plane, and she was more than glad to have a little time to unwind.

She unpacked her things and decided to indulge in a luxurious long, hot bath. She made up her mind to put all her concerns on hold for one evening. This was her last day of freedom before she received the full weight of responsibility for Laura's estate, so she might as well get the most out of it.

Chrissie was grateful to Drew for suggesting dinner. Los Angeles might be fun if one was here as a tourist and with a companion, but alone, with gnawing uncertainty, anxious about what lay ahead and having too many solitary hours to brood wasn't pleasant to contemplate.

She stepped into the bathtub, sank beneath the warm, soothing water and sighed deeply. Most likely Drew had made the offer only out of a sense of duty. She was a business client, a newly-wealthy business client, so no doubt it was part of his job to make her stay in L.A. as pleasant as possible. There was also the little matter of his feeling that he owed her a meal. Therefore, she concluded, there'd been nothing personal in the invitation.

Chrissie was annoyed at having to point that out to herself. She found Drew attractive, too attractive, but no useful purpose would be served by getting interested in the man. He seemed to like her well enough, too, but so what? Their acquaintance would be of short-term duration. She would remain in L.A. only as long as it was necessary to straighten out Laura's affairs. As soon as that was accomplished, she'd be going home to Louisiana while Drew would be here. It was important to keep that clearly in focus. She had enough problems already without inventing a new one.

Dinner with Drew was lighthearted and fun, and since she'd firmly settled the matter of not succumbing to any inappropriate interest in him, Chrissie was able to relax and enjoy his company. By an unspoken agreement, they did not discuss anything concerning the business of Chrissie's California visit.

Drew mentioned his family—his widowed mother and two brothers—and made proud boasts about his young niece and nephew. He gave colorful anecdotes about some of the pranks he and his brothers had played when they were kids. His affection for his family came through loud and clear, and Chrissie felt a tiny stab of envy because he'd had built-in playmates while growing up whereas she'd been an only child.

Still her own childhood had not been without lively companionship. There'd been cousins, lots of them on her mother's side of the family, so Chrissie, too, had her share of childhood mischief stories to tell.

Only toward the end of the evening did Drew bring up Laura's name, and then in a question concerning her adoptive family. "How is it," he asked curiously, "that your parents came in contact with Laura, seeing that they live in New Orleans and she lived here on the West Coast?"

"Dad was in the navy, stationed in San Diego at the time. A friend of theirs from Los Angeles was aware that Dad and Mom wanted to adopt because they couldn't have children of their own. He was acquainted with an attorney here who handled adoptions, so he put them in touch with him." Chrissie shrugged. "One thing led to another, and the lawyer introduced them to Laura."

"I see. What're they like—your folks?"

Chrissie smiled. "The best. Dad's sort of the strong, silent type. He doesn't talk a lot, but he's always there when I need him—from holding me steady when I was learning to ride a bike, to slipping me a couple of extra dollars over and above my allowance when I was a teenager, to changing the oil in my car to this day."

"He sounds like the type every kid deserves. My father died when I was eight, so I hardly even remember him." Drew shook off the moment of sadness, asking, "And your mother?"

Chrissie's smile widened. "Ah, she's the universal mother. She loves to cook and have a dozen people at her table; she's the first one someone calls if they're in trouble and need a hand; she'll take care of a sick friend or baby-sit one of my cousin's children or give an elderly neighbor a lift to the grocery store. It's a pity she couldn't have half a dozen kids. She had endless patience and affection."

"My mom's a little like that, too," Drew said. "Of course she's had to work ever since my dad died, so she's never had a lot of free time for much outside of her job and her family. She's had to be tough, too, to raise three rambunctious boys. But her idea of fun is when she can get the whole family together, and any occasion will do. Birthdays and anniversaries are observed, of course, but Mom'll make do with Groundhog Day or Arbor Day if she has to, if it means a dinner or a barbecue and getting everybody together." Chrissie laughed with him, and he added, "Mom's made sure to keep our family very close." Drew thought again of his mother's recent lecture. Her boys were all grown-up and on their own now, but that didn't stop her for a minute from hitting them between the eyes with some straight talk whenever it seemed called for.

The waiter arrived to see whether they wanted more coffee. Drew looked inquiringly at Chrissie.

"None for me, thanks."

"Just the check, then, please," Drew told the man. To Chrissie, he added, "It's getting late, and you're probably tired. I guess we ought to call it a night."

She nodded and admitted, "It is all sort of caving in on me."

A few minutes later they were on the way back to the hotel. Companionable silence prevailed. Drew felt no particular urge to make conversation, yet he was content. Chrissie Barrows was bright, intelligent and charming, and the more he was around her, the more he liked her. She was genuine and straightforward, and he liked that, too. It suddenly occurred to him that he hadn't been out with a woman since the breakup with Carol, yet he'd had a great time this evening. The thought was cheering. He was finally over that gloomy period of his life, and all at once he felt free, really free. He was ready for whatever the future held.

At the hotel, Drew parked and went inside with Chrissie. "I'll see you to your room," he told her as they went toward the elevator.

"It's not necessary."

"I don't mind." It was a wonderful understatement. *Mind?* Rather, he was fiercely determined to get in every last moment he could with her. Without knowing it, Chrissie had helped him to get back something of himself that Carol had taken from him. She'd helped him rediscover his normal good nature and capacity for liking both himself and life in general.

The elevator shot upward and stopped on the tenth floor. A few moments later they stood before Chrissie's door. She took her key from her purse, and Drew unlocked the door for her.

"Well...good night," she said softly. She tilted back her head and looked into his eyes. "Thanks for a wonderful evening."

"My pleasure entirely."

She was so lovely just now. Her blue eyes were a deep and mysterious shade, reflecting the rich royal blue of her silky dress. Her hair cascaded in tumbling curls to brush against her slender shoulders, and her lips were parted in a gentle smile. The dimple in her cheek played hide-and-seek, casting a spell over him.

For a long moment Drew simply absorbed the glow of her beauty, storing it in his mind for later, the way one tries to hold memories of an exquisite sunrise or a rainbow. But then, compelled by the sudden impulse of his heart, he leaned forward and kissed her.

The kiss was as light as air, as soft as rose petals. Drew's lips scarcely brushed hers, so that it had an almost misty, unreal, dreamlike effect. She tasted sweet, and her lips were infinitely soft.

He lifted his head and looked down at her in surprise. As kisses went, that fleeting contact had been practically nonexistent, yet it had done something extraordinary to him. Drew's heart pounded, and he felt a strong, relentless pull, as though he were within the circle of an invisible magnetic field. He found himself wanting more of her, a whole lot more.

Chrissie appeared as bemused as he felt. Her eyes were shuttered by wispy dark lashes, her cheeks were flushed and her lips, those warm, inviting lips, quivered ever so slightly.

Drew threw all caution to the winds. His arms went around her tiny waist, and he pulled her close. Slowly he bent his head and claimed her irresistible lips once again, and this time the kiss was one of pure fire.

It became a consuming, raging conflagration. Chrissie's lips parted beneath the pressure of his in complete surrender, and as their breaths commingled, heat poured through Drew's veins and spread in leaping flames of desire. He lost himself in the joy of her warmth, of her feminine curves pressing against his body and in the fragrance of her hair. All his senses were powerfully affected by the magic of her, and most of all, he lost himself with glad abandon in the heady excitement of her answering response.

Chrissie clung to him with her hands while her lips moved in spontaneous release to the passionate fires that stirred within her. Her body was soft and yielding, yet her hands, as they caressed his shoulders, the nape of his neck and wound through his hair, seemed to have a powerful urgency of their own that only intensified what he was feeling.

Swept up in the enchantment of her, Drew raised one hand to her breast. Through the thin silky fabric of her dress, he could feel the soft thrust of her breast, full and tender, against his fingers. An even more powerful quickening of desire spread through him.

For one long, wondrous moment, Chrissie did not resist, but then, as suddenly as the intoxicating interlude had begun, it ended. Chrissie broke the kiss and the intimate contact of their bodies by pushing her hands flat against his chest, forcing space between them. It was clearly a gesture of self-protection.

She looked stunned, knocked off balance from what had just happened. Drew himself was breathing unsteadily as he tried to bank the ardor that had ignited every nerve in his body. His head was still reeling from the frenzied emotions that had taken possession of him.

He wanted to speak, but he was unsure what to say. There was a deeply troubled expression on Chrissie's face now in place of the ungovernable feelings of a moment ago, and it sent a shiver of alarm through him.

"G-good night," she stammered in a cracked, thin thread of a voice.

Before he could find his own voice, she had already turned, fled into her room and firmly closed the door.

Drew returned to his car, but it was several minutes before he started the engine. Plain old-fashioned common sense was returning, and along with it came a scathing self-condemnation.

He had gone clean out of his mind when he'd kissed Chrissie. There was just no other explanation. She was a client, a business client, and he'd just broken a cardinal rule of the attorney-client relationship by taking far more than a professional interest in her. Why, he'd be fired from his association with Pitts, Smythe and Raleigh faster than he could blink his eyes if they ever found out! What was more, he wouldn't blame them if they did. That sizzling kiss, not to mention the liberties his hands had taken, was undoubtedly the stupidest thing he'd ever done, bar none! Why, even falling for Carol couldn't compare with it. Then he'd merely been guilty of blindness, of misjudging character, but at least he hadn't been breaching ethics!

And that disturbed expression he'd seen on Chrissie's face was evidence enough that she regretted what had happened, that she hadn't wanted it to happen. She might have been swept up by the intense sensations of the moment, but she hadn't precipitated the incident and she hadn't wanted it, so the entire blame for everything rested only on his shoulders.

Cursing himself, Drew pounded his fist against the steering wheel and gazed blankly at the hotel building for a moment. His jaw was clenched, and every muscle in his body was coiled and tense with a terrible anger for his foolish weakness.

It was a long time before he turned the key in the ignition, but when he finally left the parking lot, he raced the car down the street as though by sheer speed he could escape his monumental mistake.

Chapter Four

"Miss Barrows? I'm Linda Fields, Mr. Casey's secretary. He couldn't get away from the office at the moment, so he asked me to come for you. I hope you don't mind the substitution?"

"Not at all," Chrissie said with a smile. "I'll just get my purse." She left the young woman standing at the door and went to the dresser for her handbag.

Not having to confront Drew the first thing in the morning after the emotionally charged kiss of the night before was an unexpected but welcome reprieve. Chrissie had been nervous about seeing him again so soon, especially in the uncomfortably intimate circumstance of his calling for her at the hotel. Now she had a little breathing space before she had to encounter him, and when she did see him at the office, the meeting place itself would decree that they behave in a businesslike manner.

That kiss had seared through layers of indifference she'd had toward amorous male intentions during the past couple of years. Ever since she'd broken off with Barry, the only man she'd ever been seriously interested in, she'd felt nothing more than a mild, pleasant but unremarkable sensation whenever a man kissed her. And even Barry's kisses had never electrified her the way Drew's had done.

But just now she had neither time nor desire to dwell on such disturbing thoughts. She had a busy day ahead of her, a day in which she needed to be clearheaded and sharpwitted. With her emotions in such a chaotic state, she could only hope she would be equal to the challenges that would be presented to her.

The offices of Pitts, Smythe and Raleigh were located in an elegant, modern downtown building. Upon arrival a half hour later, Chrissie was escorted immediately into the large impressive office of one of the senior partners.

A distinguished-looking man of about sixty with neat silver hair, penetrating gray eyes and the youthful build of an athlete came forward to shake hands with her.

"I'm Bob Raleigh," he said with a welcoming smile. "It's a pleasure to meet you, Miss Barrows. My wife and I were close personal friends of your mother's—her husband, too."

Chrissie tried to smile, but failed. "It's impossible for me to think of Miss Douglas as my mother, Mr. Raleigh."

The attorney gave her a thoughtful look. "Yes. Yes, I imagine it might be. Well," he added cheerily, "please sit down. Would you like some coffee?"

"No, thank you." Chrissie took a plushly cushioned chair next to a vast window.

"That'll be all, Linda. Thank you for going to get Miss Barrows for us. Tell Drew and John she's here, will you?"

"Yes, sir."

The secretary withdrew, and Raleigh sat down on the sofa next to Chrissie's chair.

"Is all this going to be very complicated and difficult?" Chrissie asked.

Bob Raleigh smiled again. "I promise we'll do our best to make it as painless as possible. Drew Casey, whom you've already met, has been assigned the task of helping you to expedite your affairs, in addition to attempting to locate your sister. John Keene, another of our attorneys, is working hand in hand with Laura's accountant in an effort to assess the value of her holdings."

Chrissie nodded. "All of this is a bit overwhelming to me."

"I'm sure it is, but we're here to assist you in every way possible, and later on, if you have any questions or concerns about anything... anything at all, you mustn't hesitate to call us. Before you leave today, remind me to give you my home phone number so that if you ever need to call me after hours, you can reach me. As I said, my wife and I were friends with Laura, and as her daughter, you're more than just another client to me."

"Thank you, Mr. Raleigh." The man sounded sincere, and Chrissie was grateful that he seemed inclined to be of real assistance to her in her unfamiliar circumstances. Curious in spite of herself, she asked, "What was she like... really like, as a person?"

"Hmm. That's a tall order. My wife could probably fill you in better than I can. Laura was unique, kind to people she liked, but a bit of a hellcat to those she didn't. She was generous to a fault and—"

He broke off as the door opened.

Two men came in, and Bob Raleigh introduced one as John Keene. The second man was Laura's accountant. Chrissie rose to shake hands with both men, and then Drew came into the room.

She knew he was there even before she saw him. She could feel it. It was as though his very presence was a magnet that compelled a sharp awareness of him whether she liked it or not.

Chrissie turned her head to see him coming toward her. Today he wore a dark blue suit and a conservative striped blue tie. The jacket fit him well, emphasizing his powerful shoulders and long, lean torso, but it was his face that commanded her attention. It appeared somewhat drawn, and his eyes were dark and brooding. Though he wore a polite smile, his expression was somber and wary.

When he reached her, Drew clasped her hand. His fingers were cold as they touched hers, or was it her own that felt so icy? When their eyes met, she saw only rigid control. There was none of the former warmth and easy going manner he'd exhibited the other times they'd met. As for the night before—it was as though he didn't even recall it. They might be two strangers meeting for the first time.

"Good morning, Miss Barrows." Drew's handshake was brief, as though he couldn't even bear to touch her any longer than absolutely necessary.

So... it was back to formality. Chrissie felt unreasonably hurt by the curt greeting, even though a tiny shred of logic told her that in this formal business atmosphere, it was only prudence on his part. Besides, wasn't this what she wanted? A return to the impersonal, unemotional civility of two people who merely happened to be required to do business together?

"Good morning, Mr. Casey," she answered in kind, following his lead. Quickly Chrissie averted her eyes from him and returned to her chair.

The meeting began, and for the next two hours, there was much to discuss. It appeared that Laura's holdings were considerably more vast than Drew had led her to believe, and the ballpark figure of several million swelled. Chrissie's head spun as she listened to the men enumerate the possessions. There was a great deal of investment properties, from office buildings and condominiums to industrial complexes. There were stocks and bonds and part-interests in a number of businesses like restaurants and hotels; there was a horse farm in Kentucky, a ranch in Colorado, a farm in Iowa. Some of the holdings had been purchased with Laura's earnings from her movie career, but most of it had been accumulated by her husband, Martin Timms. The more the men talked, the quieter Chrissie became.

A strange sensation of suffocation began to come over her. It was as though the spacious office was devoid of fresh air, and her lungs craved oxygen. Chrissie felt an intense urge to run out of the office, outside where she could breathe and be free.

No one seemed to notice her reaction except Drew. A couple of times she was aware that he gave her an extra hard, examining look. Finally he broke in on something John Keene was saying and asked sharply, "Are you feeling all right?"

The other men fell silent, and Chrissie looked toward Drew as though he were a lifeline, forgetting that earlier she had dreaded to see him, forgetting his cold, distant manner when he first entered the office.

She shivered. "I'm...this is all a bit too much to absorb. Too...too much to be responsible for. Didn't Mr. Timms have any relatives who ought to inherit his property?"

"None," Bob Raleigh answered. "He and Laura never had any children together, and his only sister, who died before him, never married. He left everything to Laura, and she in turn left everything to you...and to your sister as well, of course, if she can be found."

"But...what am I to do?" Chrissie asked plaintively. "I don't know the first thing about handling business properties."

"There is a management firm that handles most of it," John Keene explained. "We'll set you up an appointment to see the people there in the next day or so. As for the ranch and farms, there are on-site managers who actually run things. It's really not going to be as difficult as you think, Miss Barrows. And you can always sell some of it. For instance, the ranch in Colorado really isn't a lucrative property as far as income goes. Miss Douglas kept it more out of sentiment than anything else, because her husband had been fond of it and they used to spend vacations there.''

''John's right. You'll have plenty of help and expert advice, and you'll get the hang of it sooner than you think.'' Bob Raleigh stood up and smiled at Chrissie. ''Meantime, I think we've confused you enough for one morning. I hope you'll permit me to take you to lunch. I believe Drew intends to drive you to Laura's house this afternoon. That is, if our plans meet with your approval?''

''That sounds fine.'' Chrissie was relieved to be allowed a break from so many facts and figures. Her thoughts swirled, and she needed some time to allow it all to settle down in some semblance of order in her mind.

Everyone rose, and Chrissie shook hands with John Keene and the accountant once more before they left the office. Drew nodded pleasantly at her, but did not offer to shake hands again. ''I'll meet you back here around two, and then we'll go out to Laura's place.''

Drew would've gotten out of taking Chrissie to visit the Douglas-Timms mansion if he could have figured out an acceptable way to get by with it. This morning, when he'd received an important long-distance phone call just as he was on the verge of leaving the office, he'd had a valid excuse not to pick her up at the hotel. Linda had offered to go instead, and he'd been quite pleased at how easily he'd gotten off the hook.

What hadn't been so easy was bracing himself to walk into Bob Raleigh's office and confronting Chrissie with all those other men present. He'd decided the best course of action was to behave as professionally as he could, to try to blank out everything else. He had succeeded only to the degree that outwardly he had been correctly cordial yet impersonal.

Inside, though, his emotions and self-disgust still boiled. As he left Bob Raleigh's office and went down the hall to his own, he was very relieved to get away. He could count himself lucky that Chrissie hadn't denounced his abominable behavior of last night to the boss. Drew had worked hard to get where he was, to have a coveted position with such a highly respected law firm as Pitts, Smythe and Raleigh, and he had hopes of one day being made a partner. But last night, by his irrational impulse, he could have lost it all in one fell swoop. Christina Barrows, by virtue of being Laura Douglas's daughter, was a VIP as far as Bob Raleigh was concerned. One hint in his ear from Chrissie that Drew had stepped out of line, and that would've been the end of a promising career.

It might be different if Chrissie had been flirtatious and clearly asking for a romantic gesture, but she hadn't. She'd been nothing more than friendly all evening. True, for a few moments there she'd responded with a fiery passion matching his, but the instant he'd touched her more intimately, her barriers had risen like a steel gate clanging shut. When she'd pulled away from him, she'd been upset and offended.

None of that had been evident by her manner this morning, but then neither had there been any warmth or friendliness in her greeting. Actually he'd had to admire the way she'd carried off their meeting. She'd done it with simple dignity and cool composure, so that Drew was certain that had the other men been required to testify in court of their encounter in the office, each of them would swear that Chrissie's reaction to his presence had been one of civil but emotional indifference.

When he reached his office, Drew's secretary was just preparing to go to lunch, and that reminded him that in his high state of anxiety he'd neglected to eat breakfast this morning. It was a meal he couldn't recall ever having missed before in his life. Strangely he still wasn't hungry, and he sure didn't feel like going out someplace to eat, but he decided he'd better down a little food if he intended to keep on living.

"Would you mind picking me up a sandwich on your way back?" he asked.

"What kind?" Linda asked as she held out her hand for his money.

Drew thumbed through his wallet, dug out a few bills and handed them to her. "Ham...chicken salad...anything will do."

When she was gone, Drew went inside his office, closed the door and sat down to try to figure out what he was going to say to Chrissie this afternoon when they were alone together.

As it turned out, the right opening for an apology never came. Precisely at two that afternoon, Drew returned to Bob Raleigh's office. Chrissie was waiting for him, and she gave him a pleasant nod before saying a warm goodbye to Raleigh.

She fell into step beside Drew, and they headed toward the bank of elevators. Other people were near them both in the elevator and as they walked toward his car in the parking garage, so there was no opportunity for private words.

Once they were inside the car, Chrissie asked a question concerning one of the properties that had been under discussion earlier, and Drew answered. Thus, the topic of business occupied them fully all the way to Bel Air.

While he was unable to clear the air between them, the truth was that Drew was more than happy to ignore the sensitive subject altogether. He still hadn't figured out exactly what to say. Anyway you looked at it, he'd come off looking like a jerk.

It occurred to him that maybe Chrissie was as uneasy about discussing what had happened as he was, but he had no way of knowing for sure. But a few minutes later, when Drew drove the car between two massive stone gateposts after passing the scrutiny of the electronic security camera, he saw her tense, and this time he knew he wasn't the cause of her uneasiness. She was genuinely disturbed about coming to Laura's house.

Chrissie was vaguely aware that Drew spoke—but she hadn't heard what he said, nor did she care at the moment. Her eyes were fixed on the enormous gray stone mansion ahead. It appeared to spread forever. Acres of ground surrounded the house, with trees and shrubbery and flower gardens all adding grandeur to the estate.

Drew parked in front of the wide double doors and got out. Chrissie sat still, gazing with peculiar intensity at a marble fountain some distance from the house, but she didn't see it. When Drew opened her door, she looked up at him with unhappy eyes. "I don't want to go in there."

"Why?"

"I don't belong here."

"Don't be silly." Drew's voice came, gentle yet chiding. "It's yours now."

Chrissie shook her head. "Saying so doesn't make it so."

Drew sighed. "We can leave if that's what you really want. But the staff is expecting to meet you. I let them know we were coming."

It was Chrissie's turn to sigh. In resignation she got out of the car and went up the steps.

Drew pressed the doorbell and it was answered promptly by a gray-haired lady. "Good afternoon, Mr. Casey... ma'am. Please come in."

Chrissie stepped inside. The large foyer boasted an Italian tile floor, a large gilded mirror and a dark, highly polished table on which rested a bowl of flowers.

"Alice, I'd like you to meet Christina Barrows, Miss Douglas's daughter."

The woman extended her hand and said cordially, "It's so nice to meet you." She tilted her head to one side assessingly and smiled. "You have Miss Laura's mouth for sure. And her delicate cheekbones."

Chrissie was somewhat startled. "I suppose I would have some of her features, wouldn't I?" The thought did not make her happy even though they were speaking of one of the most acclaimed beauties of modern times.

"Please come into the library and I'll bring tea. The rest of the staff is eager to meet you, too."

Chrissie allowed herself to be ushered into the library. It was a large cheerful room with a stone fireplace at one end. The hearth was filled with a basket of spring flowers. Walls were lined with bookshelves filled with elegant bound books and bric-a-brac.

Once they were alone, Chrissie said to Drew, "I'm a little surprised by this room. The public image of Laura wasn't exactly that of a bookish woman."

"Nor was she," another feminine voice said. Chrissie turned toward the door to see a woman of about thirty-five enter the room. She had short brown hair, intelligent eyes and a friendly manner. She extended her hand toward Chrissie as she spoke. "This was really Mr. Timms's room, but after his death, Miss Douglas used it as her office. I'm Jane White. I was Miss Douglas's personal secretary."

"I see. I had no idea she had a secretary," Chrissie said as they shook hands. "I hope you'll stay on and help me go through all her papers and household possessions."

Jane White nodded briskly. "I'm more than happy to help out as long as you need me. By the way, will you be

wanting to stay here in the house while you're in town? Mr.
Casey,'' she went on, indicating Drew by a nod of her head,
''said you'd asked him to book you into a hotel, but we can
make a room ready for you immediately if you want.''

''Not just yet. Maybe later.'' Chrissie realized the hotel
room was a needless extravagance, but she couldn't bring
herself to simply waltz in and make free of Laura's home.
Perhaps she was being silly, but she just couldn't do it.

Alice brought the tea, followed by two people who were
introduced as the daily maid and the gardener. Chrissie did
her awkward best, thanking them for all they'd done on
Laura's behalf, and was glad when they departed.

Jane White remained, calmly sitting down and pouring
out the tea while Drew and Chrissie took their places on a
sofa. The secretary was clearly in charge, yet she was not
pushy or aggressive; rather, she had a matter-of-fact sensible manner that Chrissie liked.

''The staff is wondering how much longer they'll all have
their jobs,'' she said as she handed Chrissie a cup. Smiling
in a forthright way, she added, ''I'm among their number,
of course.''

Chrissie's eyes briefly met Drew's as though she were
asking for help. Yet she knew he couldn't help her in this
situation. It was her problem and no one else's.

''I wish I could give you a firm answer,'' she replied,
carefully choosing her words. ''But I only just arrived, you
know, and there are many things I'm going to have to consider. I probably will be putting this place on the market—
I have no use for it myself since I live in New Orleans. But I
would like to have the staff remain until such time as it's sold
so that they could keep everything in top condition.''
Chrissie's gaze wavered as she tried to choose the right
words. Her newfound role certainly was keeping her on her
toes. ''On the other hand, I understand the need for job security. Please tell everyone for me that I'll continue to pay

their salaries for as long as I require their services, if they choose to remain until then. If anyone locates another job in the meantime and wants to leave sooner, I quite understand. All I can promise is that when I do finally close the house, I'll be as generous as possible with termination checks for anyone who's still with me.''

"That sounds fair enough," Jane White said.

The three of them chatted casually over their tea, and the secretary mentioned that she'd been with Laura Douglas for eight years.

"Did you enjoy working for such a well-known celebrity?"

Jane shrugged. "It had its ups and downs like any job, but for the most part Laura was a good employer. She didn't make excessive demands as a rule, and she was normally considerate. I'm sorry she's gone, and not just because it means I'll be looking for another job soon, either." She gave Chrissie a thoughtful glance. "I'm sorry, too, that you never got to meet her."

"There was never any question of that happening," Chrissie answered shortly. "The truth was deliberately kept from me."

Drew, as though trying to distract her from the direction her bitter thoughts were leading, set his cup down with a clatter on the low table next to him and said to the other woman, "I think Miss Barrows would probably like to see the rest of the house."

"Of course." Jane White stood up. "I'll show you around now."

Drew turned to Chrissie. "I'll wait outside."

Sudden panic assailed her, and she asked, almost pleading, "Don't you want to come with us?"

"It's a rather personal tour," he said softly. "I think you'll probably do better without me." He turned, shook hands with the secretary and left the room.

Chrissie drained her cup and rose, knowing she couldn't postpone the inevitable any longer. A moment later she, too, left the library, reluctantly trailing along behind Jane White and trying not to think how much she must resemble a vulture come to pick the flesh off the bones.

Undoubtedly Laura's home was the most beautiful private residence Chrissie had ever seen. There was a palatial-sized living room with wide expanses of glass to include the walled garden just beyond. Sofas and chairs were upholstered in beige silk, and Austrian shades on the windows were a patterned beige. The floor boards were wide planks, and dark beams across the slanted ceiling picked up the deep brown tone. Against this beige-and-brown background, the bright colors of rugs, pillows, tall Oriental vases and large plants provided splashes of cheer.

On the ground floor, in addition to the kitchen and formal dining room, there was an exercise room and a small den that was also a film projection room. "All of Miss Douglas's own films are here, of course," Jane explained, "but there are also many others spanning the past two decades. She enjoyed watching movies, but though they tell me Mr. Timms watched her films, Laura didn't like to see her own performances."

When they were back in the central hall, Jane pointed toward a closed door and said, "My office is in there. And just off the kitchen are Alice's private rooms."

"Does everyone on staff live in?" Chrissie asked.

"Only Alice. I have a bedroom upstairs that I used sometimes whenever there was a need for me to stay overnight, but I live in an apartment a few miles from here." Jane led Chrissie up the curving staircase and said, "The house has ten bedrooms and twelve baths, counting Alice's rooms."

Chrissie gasped. "Why so many? Laura and her husband didn't even have children."

"I understand they used to entertain a great deal when Mr. Timms was alive. Since I've been here, all of the bedrooms have never been occupied at one time. Sometimes Miss Douglas had overnight guests, but her entertaining tended to be the cocktail or dinner party variety rather than weekend parties."

Chrissie took a brief glimpse into each of the upstairs bedrooms, including the one Jane used. Each one was a piece of art with a definite color scheme, a period or an ethnic theme. A Mexican room had bright mosaic tile, stucco walls and massive dark furniture; an Early American room with warm brown woods and copper bowls; a Versailles room with parquet flooring and Louis Quinze furnishings.

"This," Jane said as they reached a door at the end of the long hall, "was Miss Douglas's room." She opened the door and stood back.

Taking a deep breath, Chrissie forced herself to step across the threshold. The room was a curious yet beautiful blend of ultramodern clean lines and country-style floral. The bed and tables were brass and glass, evoking a sense of order and spaciousness. The comforter on the bed was shell-pink satin above a floral dust ruffle. The same floral chintz was picked up by a wing-back chair and ottoman and in the colors used in several pastel watercolor paintings of flowers. It was an exquisitely lovely room, homey, yet sleek and uncluttered.

Chrissie experienced the choking feeling once more. Without going farther into the room, she simply turned, brushed past Jane White and walked away.

"I'm sorry if seeing her room upset you," the secretary said as she hurriedly followed Chrissie toward the stairs. "We could have skipped it if you'd told me."

"That's all right." Chrissie was already feeling better by the time she reached the stairs. Nevertheless she'd had enough of Laura's house for one day. "I'll be going now," she said firmly as she descended the stairs.

"What about..." Jane White hesitated until they reached the foot of the stairs. "What about going through her things, Miss Barrows? I suppose if it bothers you, I could do it alone, but..."

"No. No. I'll do it. I *will* do it," Chrissie added firmly. "I just need a little time, that's all. I'll try to come back tomorrow, and if not then, the following day, and we can get started." She shook hands with the secretary and left the house, eager to escape.

Drew was lounging next to the car. He stood up straight when he saw her coming toward him. "You look a little pale," he said thoughtfully. "Are you all right?"

"I'm fine. It was just...a bit hard, that's all. Can we go now?"

Drew opened the door for her, and in another minute they were driving through the gate. Only when they were well away from the mansion did Chrissie feel as though she could breathe freely again.

They were silent most of the way back to the hotel, and Chrissie was grateful that Drew wasn't in a talkative mood. She was having a difficult time getting a grip on her emotions—awe, nervousness, a softening, and contrarily, a hardening resentment.

But at length, she broke the silence herself. "You haven't said today...has there been any new word concerning Victoria?"

"No. I'm sorry."

Chrissie sighed. "It doesn't seem like enough—just to sit here and wait while someone else searches...if that attorney in London really is searching."

Drew fell silent for a moment, then said, "Okay. If it'll make you feel any better, I'll go to England myself in a couple of weeks if Chamberlain's still drawing a blank by then."

Chrissie nodded. "It would. But if it comes to that, I intend to make the trip with you."

Drew was immediately and vehemently against the idea. "It won't be necessary for both of us to go."

"Then you stay here and *I'll* go," Chrissie said adamantly. "After all, she's *my* sister, and I'm more eager to find her than you are—or this Bill Chamberlain you hired to search for her. To both of you, this is only another assignment, merely another job but to me it's the most important search in the world!"

Drew didn't respond. They were in heavy traffic now, so he applied all his attention to his driving. Even so, he couldn't help mulling over Chrissie's intention to accompany him to England if a trip became necessary.

It was the last thing he wanted. He didn't understand all the feelings that Chrissie evoked in him, but whether he liked it or not, she affected him in a very profound way every time they were together. That first evening in her apartment he'd been drawn to her like the proverbial moth to flame; then look what had happened last night! Today, thank heaven, they hadn't been in circumstances that permitted him such an ill-considered, rash act as to kiss her, but that hadn't stopped him from caring about her. He'd become concerned during the meeting this morning when she'd grown so quiet and pale, as though all the information the men were relaying to her was a bombardment of stones. He'd had a swift, instinctive desire to protect her from them—pretty dumb, actually, since those men had hardly been abusing her. But there it was. And then during the past hour at Laura's house, that protective feeling toward her had reared up again when he'd seen how reluctant she was even to go inside the house. He'd wanted to put his arms around her and hold her until that wan, lost look vanished from her face, and the intensity of his feelings had disturbed him. That was why he'd excused himself from going through the mansion with her and Laura's secretary. If Chrissie broke down, it was better if he wasn't there to see it, because in his present state, he wasn't sure he could maintain a proper professional distance.

When she'd come out of the house, he'd noticed at once that her eyes were bright and glassy, as though tears were dangerously close, and again he'd felt a strange longing to take her into his arms and comfort her. Drew was beginning to realize that he couldn't trust his own emotions, his own actions, and the near loss of control was deeply unsettling. So—if he ended up having to visit England, he certainly didn't want Chrissie along. She was too damned tempting as it was, and he shuddered to think what it would be like for him if he had to travel with her and be in her company on a continual basis.

Yet he didn't know how he could prevent it, either. He wasn't her boss; if she wanted to make a rather fine point of it, as his client, she was actually *his* boss.

Traffic finally thinned, the car shot forward, and in three short blocks Drew pulled into the driveway at the entrance of the hotel. He put the gear into park, got out and walked around the car as a bellman came to open Chrissie's door.

The bellman moved away once Chrissie got out, and for a long moment Drew and Chrissie simply stood there gazing at each other. Chrissie had that vulnerable lost expression on her face again, and Drew was glad they were standing in an open public place so that discretion would force him to refrain from touching her.

"Thanks for all your help," Chrissie said softly.

"There's no need for that," he answered with a tiny smile. "About your idea, Chrissie—honestly there's no reason both of us should go to London if we decide it's necessary for anyone to go. The search could take a long time, and it would only be tedious and frustrating for you. Wait until we actually locate her, and then—"

Chrissie shook her head and interrupted. "If Mr. Chamberlain hasn't turned up any leads by the end of next week, I'm going. While school is out for the summer, I've got the free time right now to travel, and according to what all you lawyers have told me," she said dryly, "I have the financial resources. I can't think of a better way to use some of Laura's money than by trying to find my sister. And if I do decide I have to go, I *know* I'll be diligent in the search."

"Meaning we won't?" Drew sighed. "I promise, if I go I'll be just as diligent as you would. Besides, you're going to have enough to attend to here settling the estate."

Chrissie shrugged indifferently. "I'll just put everything on hold. Finding Victoria is more important than a hundred stuffy old business meetings or studying boring legal papers."

There was going to be no talking her out of it. Drew had run out of arguments. So much for being a good court attorney! He couldn't even wear down one surprisingly strong-willed young woman! "All right," he said at last, trying to be as gracious as he could in defeat, "all right. Do you have a passport?"

"Yes. I went to Europe a couple of years ago with some friends. I brought it along with me just in case."

Drew gave her a hard stare. "You've been planning to go all the time!" he accused.

Chrissie grinned. "Well... only if you and Chamberlain don't find her soon. But I figured I couldn't go wrong by being prepared."

Drew didn't argue any further. It seemed pointless. He said goodbye to Chrissie, and when he drove away, his only hope was that a miracle would happen and Bill Chamberlain would locate the missing twin during the next few days. But then his mouth twisted grimly. With his sort of luck, the next thing he knew, he'd be on a plane to London with Chrissie right beside him, looking devastatingly lovely and vulnerable and tempting him beyond endurance.

He was afraid he was as good as fired from Pitts, Smythe and Raleigh already.

Chapter Five

Chrissie was utterly despondent as she entered her hotel room. She had found the morning business discussions tedious; then the afternoon visit to Laura's house had been emotionally draining. There was a lump in her throat the size of a grapefruit, and she still felt on the verge of tears.

All in all, she concluded as she began to shed her clothes, it had been a very depressing day. It had started out badly because of her dread at seeing Drew again after that startling kiss last night. She was still shocked at her own intense response, at how quickly things had gotten out of hand. It was embarrassing and unnerving. True, the kiss had taken her by surprise, but once it had begun, it had been up to her to bring it to a hasty end, which, to her everlasting shame, she hadn't done. She'd let things go to dangerous extremes, and once she'd finally had enough willpower to pull away from him, there'd been no way she could salvage her self-respect. All she'd been able to do was make a cowardly retreat.

This morning when they'd met in Bob Raleigh's office, it had been obvious that Drew also regretted what had gone on between them. He'd been cold and distant as though he blamed her. As if that weren't bad enough, Raleigh had sent them off together to the Douglas-Timms mansion. Chrissie had cringed with dread at being alone with Drew in his car, so she'd done the only thing she could think of—she'd distracted him with business questions so that there would be no opportunity for any personal comments.

By the time they'd gotten to the mansion, she was feeling more comfortable with him, and once there, she'd been deeply glad he was with her. Even though he'd opted out from going along to tour the house, somehow she'd felt strengthened by his silent support, and on the drive back to the hotel afterward, he'd been kind.

Until she'd expressed her intention to go to England. Chrissie was a little puzzled by his objection. What difference did it make to Drew?

It didn't matter anyway, she decided obstinately as she stepped into the shower. She had to do what she thought best, and if she had to search the British Isles from one end to the other, she would do it. Now that she knew she had a twin, she was obsessed with finding her, and she didn't care what anyone else thought she ought to do.

Chrissie turned, allowing the hot water to beat against her shoulders and back. She still had such mixed emotions about Laura Douglas being her mother, about suddenly inheriting all her wealth. Now she was a rich woman, but she could find no pleasure in the thought. The concept didn't even seem real. This morning she'd felt remote, as though all the talk during the meeting was going to affect someone else's life, not her own. Later, inside Laura's house, she'd felt ghoulish, like a thief, an interloper. The woman they said was her mother had never been anything to her personally, so what right did she now have to suddenly walk in and take possession of everything that had belonged to a complete stranger? It felt wrong.

Chrissie soaped her body and then scrubbed vigorously with a washcloth, but no amount of scrubbing and rinsing could wash away her feelings. Her animosity ran deep toward the woman who had not only given her away, but who had coldheartedly, deliberately denied her any knowledge of or association with her father and twin sister. Gratitude for her sizable inheritance was literally beyond her.

She finished the shower, toweled dry and padded into the bedroom, wishing she could talk to her parents. Right now in the lonely splendor of her elegant hotel room, she could use a little down-to-earth sanity, not to mention encouragement. But Jack and Marie were somewhere between New Orleans and Denver, and it was impossible to reach them. And anyway, they'd promised to call her on Saturday.

Chrissie slipped on a pair of shorts and a shirt and then, to escape the oppressive silence of the hotel room, stepped out onto her balcony. It overlooked the enormous kidney-shaped swimming pool below.

There was only one couple in the pool just now, and they appeared to be about Chrissie's own age. They also were clearly very much in love. They played and cavorted and laughed and kissed, and swallowing hard, Chrissie turned away and went back into her room.

If only she had someone of her own who loved her and who would help her get through these difficult and rather intimidating circumstances. But there was no one.

There'd only been one man she'd been serious about, and what a whopper of a mistake that had been! Barry was an entrepreneur on whom she'd wasted a solid year of her life. He'd had a terrific personality, which had been one of his chief attractions; he'd been ambitious to succeed in life, which at first had been another attraction. But though he'd sworn he loved her and wanted to spend his life with her,

Barry could never be pinned down to set a wedding date. He'd wanted his financial affairs to be perfect before he took on the responsibility of a wife and family. He'd insisted on X amount of dollars in his savings account, but once he'd reached that goal, he had decided to buy a piece of investment property first. When that was paid off, there'd been something else to take its place. Chrissie had finally been forced to accept the fact that Barry loved business success and the pursuit of money far more than he could ever love a woman.

Humorlessly she thought how strange it was, the way things turned out. Here she was, an unwilling multimillionaire without having lifted a finger, while Barry was still eagerly chasing the almighty dollar to the exclusion of any personal life of his own. If he'd only married her when he'd had the chance, he could have closed his grasping fingers around everything she'd just inherited! It was a delicious irony. He would probably be sick with despair if he ever found out.

Thinking along those lines, Chrissie was brought up short. It came to her in a sudden, unpleasant jolt that from now on she would have to consider greed as a possible motive whenever any man showed an interest in her.

That fiery, passionate kiss with Drew—it had been so unexpected. Could it be that he was like Barry, that he'd had money on his mind when he'd seemed to take such a sudden, unexpected romantic interest in her?

It was a sickening idea. She didn't want to think such things, yet the possibility, however faint, existed, and she had to consider it.

But if that were the case, why had he done such an about-face today? Had he gotten cold feet about what he was doing and decided that even with so much money for the pickings, making love to a woman he didn't care about just wasn't worth it? Chrissie hoped Drew had some integrity, that if all he saw were dollar signs when he looked at her, he would make no more moves toward her. All the same, it hurt to imagine that might be all that had attracted him to her. She had liked him very much from the beginning, and the memory of the kiss last night could still make her bones melt.

Sighing, Chrissie decided the best thing she could do was to put everything out of her mind. She went to the telephone, ordered dinner from room service and tried to call her friend Jim in New Orleans just to hear a friendly voice. All she got was his answering machine. Chrissie left a message, then hung up. In desperation she flipped on the television and tried not to think about how boring the long evening ahead would be.

Drew had a bit of business to complete on a different case he was wrapping up, so the next morning, although he knew Chrissie was on the premises of the law office, he was able to stay hidden away in his own suite. Today John Keene was responsible for her. He was scheduled to take her to Laura's bank to open the safety deposit box, and afterward to a luncheon meeting with some of the people from the investment management firm.

Drew was glad of the breather. He'd become far more attracted to Chrissie than was good for him, so it was better all around if he could avoid seeing her any more than was strictly necessary.

Thinking about Chrissie reminded him of her surprising announcement of her intention to accompany him to England to search for her sister. Drew was still adamantly against the idea, and with the possibility lodged ominously in his mind, he pushed aside the papers on his desk, which he wasn't having much luck keeping his attention on anyway, and scooped up the telephone.

"Get me Bill Chamberlain in London," he told his secretary.

"Yes, sir."

Drew drummed his fingers impatiently on his desk as he waited for the call to be put through, but when his buzzer finally sounded and he picked up the phone once more, Linda said, "Mr. Chamberlain's already left his office for the day."

"Damn!"

Drew knew it was a cockeyed notion, but he'd been hoping for a miracle somehow—that Bill would say he'd already located the missing Victoria, that he was putting her on a plane for L.A., that there was no reason in the world why Drew and Chrissie both should make a trip to England. So much for miracles.

Still, maybe something would break during the next few days. You never knew. Drew tried to be optimistic. He also tried to get back to work and get his mind off Chrissie instead of wondering how she'd spent her evening last night after he left her at the hotel.

As for himself, he'd gone home to suffer through a bad temper because he was alone, because all there was to eat for dinner was a frozen dinner, which he overcooked in the oven to a fine crispy black-brown, and because he kept remembering the night before when he'd enjoyed a fine meal in Chrissie's company. But then he'd blown it with that kiss, and he hadn't dared invite her to dinner again.

He'd feared if he did, the situation might very well get out of hand again. Chrissie attracted him like a moth to flame. Yet Drew realized she was in a vulnerable state right now, what with all the major shocks and adjustments she'd had to deal with recently, and she needed someone she could lean on and trust. If he followed his growing inclinations to attempt to make love to her, and if she responded, would it be because she was equally attracted to him, or simply because she needed somebody?

And what about his own emotional state? He liked to think he was one hundred percent recovered from Carol's treachery, but was he really? Or was at least some of what he was feeling toward Chrissie based on the old rebound theory? Drew truly did not think that was the case, but he wanted to be perfectly clear about that in his own mind before he got involved in any new relationship.

Therein lay the crux of the matter. Chrissie was under too much stress right now to make a sensible commitment to anyone, even supposing she wanted such a relationship with him, while he needed to be certain that his own emotional slate was clean. Christina Barrows was first-class, a fine person, the sort of woman a man treated fairly, with honorable intent. She wasn't a good-time party girl you could wave goodbye to without compunction after a few dates, so for both their sakes, Drew had to be sure of what he was doing before he started anything.

Drew sighed. His chaotic woolgathering was making his head ache. And defining the problem had not brought with it a satisfying resolution. He bent his head over the papers on his desk and attempted to concentrate, but he was interrupted by the buzzer.

"Yes?"

"Your mother is on line four," Linda informed him.

"Thanks."

Drew punched the lighted button and leaned back in his chair. "Hi, Mom," he said warmly. "What's up?"

"Dinner tonight. I know it's short notice, but can you make it? Everyone else will be here."

Drew knew "everyone else" meant his two brothers and their families. At least once a month his mother tried to get them all together. "Sure," he said in answer to her question. "I'm free as the breeze tonight."

His mother sighed heavily in his ear. "That's too bad. I was hoping you'd tell me you had a date."

"Now, Mom," Drew began with a quick flash of irritation. "You know that subject's—"

"Off-limits. I know. I know. You'll start dating again when you're good and ready and not before. But tonight *is* Friday night, so I kind of hoped maybe there was a chance you'd already made plans."

The best defense was a good offense. Drew gave it a try. "If you don't want me to come to dinner tonight, why did you bother to invite me?" He injected his voice with as much trumped-up injury as he could.

"You *know* that's not what I meant!" his mother gasped. "Drew, how could you even think it? Of course I want you to come tonight! I'm sorry if I gave you the wrong impression!"

Drew grinned at the telephone receiver. The ploy had worked. Now he had his mother sputtering apologies for having hurt his sensitive feelings; meantime, she'd gotten off his case, which had been his objective. "I'll forgive you if you'll let me have second helpings of dessert," he teased.

But after they rang off, he was glumly conscious of what his mother had so bluntly pointed out—that it was Friday, he was single, young, fairly presentable, and yet his romantic life was so dry that he had nothing better to do than spend the evening with his family.

Carol was out of his life, and good riddance, but since then he hadn't attempted to get back into circulation. That had more to do with distaste for the senseless revolving wheel of the dating scene than from any lingering feelings toward his ex-fiancée. But regardless of his reasons, his mother had made a valid point. He hadn't been put on this earth to be a monk. Besides, if he'd had a more well-rounded social life, he probably never would've overstepped the bounds of propriety with Chrissie Barrows in the first place. After all, she wasn't really *that* exceptional or unique. Drew knew lots of women who were prettier, who had equally pleasing personalities.

No...the whole problem stemmed from having made himself too much of a hermit of late. His self-imposed solitude had upset his equilibrium. Definitely sometime very soon, he concluded, he was going to have to make a serious effort to meet some new women.

Chrissie gazed at her reflection in the mirror with cool objectivity and finally decided she was satisfied. The white silky dress was flattering to her figure with its narrow skirt, V-neckline and full, flowing sleeves. At her waist was an intricately beaded white-and-gold belt. The dress was both elegant and demurely understated, just the thing for her dinner tonight with Bob Raleigh and his wife.

Raleigh had issued the invitation this morning before she left with John Keene for her rounds to the bank and a visit to the management firm that handled many of Laura's commercial properties. She had been pleased by the suggestion because it would be a far more entertaining way of spending the evening than dining alone in her room as she'd done the previous night.

A moment later there was a knock on the door. Chrissie glanced at her watch. 6:10. Bob Raleigh had promised to come for her at 6:15. She quickly gave her hair one last pat, picked up her small white evening bag and went toward the door.

"You're very prompt," she said, opening the door. Abruptly she fell silent and stared in amazement. The caller wasn't the older man she'd been expecting. Instead it was Drew...a Drew she hadn't seen before.

He'd shed the formality of suits and ties for faded jeans, a corn-yellow polo shirt and sneakers. One bare arm stretched out before him at an angle as his hand braced against the door facing. His stance was one of utter relaxation.

"Hi," he said.

"Hi, yourself."

Chrissie swallowed and tried to beat down the swift delight that fluttered through her at the sight of him here at her door. It was the last thing she'd expected, since she hadn't even had a glimpse of him today when she'd been at the law office.

Drew's gaze flickered over her in frank appraisal. All at once Chrissie became breathless, conscious that his dark eyes seemed to remain fixed overlong on the low neckline.

In an effort to distract him—and herself—she asked somewhat huskily, "What are you doing here?" Yet somehow it didn't seem to matter at all. She was just glad he was.

Reluctantly Drew forced himself to look away from the enthralling glimpse of the dusky hollow visible between her breasts. It should have been easier for him to think clearly once he was gazing at Chrissie's face, but somehow that didn't happen. There he confronted her lips, those same lovely ruby-red lips that had been so warm on his two nights ago right here at this very door. The memory caught in his throat, tantalizing and disturbing. So much for entertaining the thought of other, prettier women. All he cared about was this one.

When he finally spoke again, his voice was deep and strained. "There's been a change of plans."

"What plans?"

"Your dinner plans with the Raleighs. Bob called me a few minutes ago and asked me to come and make his apologies. They just received word that their son was involved in a car accident."

"How awful!" Chrissie gasped. "Is it serious?"

"It didn't sound too serious, but they are going to be running some tests at the hospital. Naturally Bob and his wife want to be there."

"Naturally." Chrissie nodded, then added, "But you didn't need to make a trip to the hotel to tell me. You could've just phoned."

Drew shook his head. "Nope. I said there'd been a change of plans, not a complete cancellation. You'll be coming to dinner with me instead. How does some home cooking strike you?"

Chrissie tilted her head and gave a mock shudder. "Is scorched water on the menu?"

Drew grinned. "You're leaping to conclusions again. Did I say whose home or whose cooking?"

"Well..."

"We're going to my mother's house."

Chrissie was surprised at the suggestion. Taking a girl home to Mom was something a man did with someone he cared about, not a mere business client...even if he had kissed... She shook her head and nixed the idea at once. "I can't possibly intrude on your mother."

"She's already being intruded upon to the tune of three sons, two daughters-in-law and two grandchildren. One person more or less won't make any difference at all. With our gang, Mom's used to cooking enough food for a small army."

"Even so, I can't just show up at her table when she's not expecting me."

"She'll be perfectly happy to have you, so I won't take no for an answer. Now shake a leg and get changed. That's one smashing dress...." Briefly his gaze swept downward over her luscious form a last time. "But take my word for it, you don't want to wear it around my lovable but messy niece and nephew. You got any jeans with you?"

Slightly bemused, Chrissie nodded.

"Then hop to it. I'll wait for you out here." Drew pulled the door closed between them.

While he waited for her, Drew paced the hall. He couldn't decide for sure whether he was glad he'd be spending the evening with Chrissie or not, but no doubt it would cheer his mother. Chrissie was female, young, single and very good-looking. Even learning Chrissie was only a client wasn't likely to disappoint Mom. She wasn't looking to marry him off in the near future so much as she simply wanted him to exhibit the signs of a normal man enjoying the company of a lovely woman.

And how did he feel himself? Drew reached the fire exit, did a military precision about-face and stalked along the corridor back toward Chrissie's door. One part of him wanted to throw all caution to hell, take her into his arms and repeat the fervent kiss of the other evening, but a more cautious part of him advised that such a move would be just about the stupidest thing he could do. The feelings he had for Chrissie probably weren't legitimate, and the last thing he wanted was for either of them to be hurt. Tonight he was determined to keep things light and casual. With all her recent shocks, Chrissie didn't need romantic pressures from a guy who didn't know his own mind.

Chrissie was rather amused at herself over how readily she complied with the order to "hop to it." Without the slightest bit of regret, she discarded dress, panty hose and pumps in favor of jeans, a comfortable oversized white cotton shirt and sandals. She was sorry that the Raleighs' son had been injured in an accident, but she couldn't be sorry over the prospect of spending the evening with Drew instead of the law firm's senior partner and his wife. The plan had seemed agreeable enough when it was all that had been open to her, but it seemed dull and flat next to an evening with Drew and his family. She didn't allow herself to stop and dwell upon the ramifications of why that was so. It simply was. Suddenly she looked forward to the evening ahead with a great deal of anticipation.

When Chrissie emerged from her room, she paused for the briefest instant as her eyes met Drew's. Something flickered in her gaze, something that was there one moment and gone the next, but he caught its meaning and was abruptly heartened despite his hands-off resolution. It had been a spark of undisguised pleasure. A smile came to Drew's lips. "Ready?"

"Ready."

There was no lingering trace of awkwardness between them. The tension of yesterday was gone, and as they set out laughing and joking, it was easy for them both to feel an optimistic pleasure concerning the unexpected evening ahead in each other's company.

Thirty minutes later Drew parked his car in front of his mother's unpretentious house in the foothills of the San Fernando Mountains. Single-handedly, since her husband had died over twenty years before, his mother had raised three sons. She had worked hard to support them, taught them values and prodded them to do their best in school. The result was that all three sons had received college scholarships. Now one son was a physician, one a business-man and one an attorney. Yet nothing had come easily for any of them, least of all Drew's mother. In Drew's book, any woman who could pull off all she'd done and still have a sense of humor and a love of life was a super human being. It was with genuine pride that he brought Chrissie to meet his mother, as well as his brothers.

Inside the house, Drew made the introductions, and he was aboveboard about Chrissie's identity as a client and forthcoming about the last-minute arrangements that had brought her here with him tonight. He didn't want any er-roneous assumptions on anybody's part. Still he couldn't help but experience a definite satisfaction from the fact that

Chrissie was with *him*, standing at *his* side, meeting *his* family. It felt good.

As she met each member of Drew's family, Chrissie tried hard to keep everyone's name straight in her mind. First there was his mother. Maggie Casey had short iron-gray hair, but the untouched gray was the only giveaway that she was actually old enough to have three grown sons in their thirties. She had the lithe, slender build and quick, energetic movements of a teenaged girl, a warm, firm handshake and best of all, laughing eyes. Chrissie liked her on sight. In quick succession, she met the others—Bruce, the doctor, his wife, Ann, and their children, Lisa, age three and Brian, eighteen months. Then there was David and his bride, Susan.

"It's a pleasure to meet you, Chrissie," Maggie said, giving her hand a friendly pat.

"I'm sorry about just showing up this way," Chrissie said. "I'm sure it's a bother, but Drew insisted it was all right."

"It's perfectly fine," Maggie warmly assured her. "I always like to meet my son's special friends."

"I'm only a client." Chrissie felt it was her duty to emphasize the point.

"Hmm. Yes." An impish smile darted across Maggie's face. "What I want to know, then, is how does my son rate a client as lovely as you are? And I always thought the law was so dull!"

Chrissie felt her face turning pink. "You're too kind," she murmured in embarrassment.

"No. She's just too outspoken and likes to tease too much," Drew said tartly. He cast a quelling glance in his mother's direction. He could take her teasing at his own expense, but he wasn't sure how Chrissie felt about it.

Maggie grinned unrepentantly, but her next words were mild enough as she released Chrissie's hand. "I'm delighted you could join us tonight, my dear. And you are very lovely, whether my son likes my saying so or not! Now, if you'll excuse me, I'd better check on my roast.''

Drew led Chrissie to the sofa, where she sat down next to David and Susan. ''So you're from New Orleans?'' asked Dave. ''I always thought Creole girls had dark hair and eyes.''

''Some of them do,'' Chrissie replied easily. ''My mom is a classic example, but I was adopted.''

''Ah. Well, are they really as beautiful as they're reputed to be?''

Before Chrissie could frame a reply, Dave's bride was playfully punching him in the solar plexus. ''It's none of your business if they are,'' Susan informed him. ''If we ever go to New Orleans, I'll make you wear blinders.''

Chrissie considered the attractive blonde and laughed. ''I wouldn't worry if I were you.''

The evening sped by quickly as though each hour wore wings. Chrissie found to her astonishment that she enjoyed every minute. She seemed to fit right into the easygoing, good-natured group as though she actually belonged. Bruce and Dave joked that it was a pity she was stuck with such incompetent legal counsel as their brother; they offered to help her find a knowledgeable first-year law student to take his place. Maggie was interested and sympathetic over the story of Chrissie's missing twin sister, and both Ann and Susan seemed to take to her right away and she to them, the way people do sometimes for no accountable reason at all.

Even Bruce and Ann's young children seemed to like Chrissie. Little Brian allowed her to hold him on her lap while Lisa cuddled up next to her on the sofa after dinner and Chrissie told them a story. It was a little saga she'd made up herself to entertain her students at school. The tale included such characters as a snobby pelican, a bashful alligator and three ornery crayfish, and it involved a lot of hand motions and pantomimes. The two youngsters listened intently, trying to mimic Chrissie's words and movements.

Drew watched with a mixture of pride, astonishment and bittersweet enjoyment. The entire family had taken to Chrissie, and now the rest of the adults, like himself, were as enthralled by her entertaining yarn as the children themselves.

The contrast between this evening and the times he'd brought Carol was stark, and yet if Drew had been required to say exactly what the difference was, he'd have been hard put to do it. His brothers had always been polite to Carol, but they'd never joked with her as though she were just one of the gang the way they did with Chrissie. He couldn't have put his finger on precisely why, but somehow he could tell that his sisters-in-law both genuinely liked Chrissie, too, whereas their relationship with Carol had always been somewhat strained and the friendliness more forced than natural.

Even his mother was making a fuss in her nonfussing way, simply by virtue of having allowed Chrissie into her kitchen. Except for her daughters-in-law, Drew couldn't remember her ever allowing a visitor to lift a finger there before. Maggie had always considered her kitchen a special, near-hallowed domain, reserved only for her nearest and dearest. Yet she'd permitted Chrissie along with Susan and Ann to help with the cleaning-up after dinner. From the living room where he'd been banished along with his brothers, Drew had heard an awful lot of laughing going on, as if all the females in the house were having a private party.

When Chrissie finished telling her story to the children, Lisa begged for another, but her father intervened. "It's getting late, sweetheart, and we need to get you and your brother home to bed," Bruce said. "How about thanking

Chrissie for telling you the story and saying good-night to everyone?''

The little girl complied and gave Chrissie a hug. "Will you come back to see us again and tell us another story?"

Chrissie laughed gently, but before she replied, she looked across the room at Drew as though by instinct. Her gaze had a powerful impact on him. It caught at his breath and sent a tiny current of electricity through him. She was so lovely sitting there with the children in her arms, so natural in her manner with them, and it suddenly occurred to Drew that he was waiting for her response to his niece's question just as though the answer was of paramount importance. Their gazes locked in a strange, fiercely intense manner for a long moment... hot, mesmerizing, consuming.

Finally Chrissie broke the contact. She looked down at the little girl beside her with an odd, unfathomable smile on her lips. "Perhaps," she said at length. "We'll see."

At least she hadn't given an outright no. Drew wasn't sure exactly what was happening to him, but he felt hope swelling inside him. For some inexplicable reason, it seemed to matter, to matter a lot whether Chrissie wanted to be among his family again. Because if she did, it would also mean she wanted to be with him, as well.

During the course of the evening, Drew had somehow managed to forget all his logical objections to his strengthening attraction to Chrissie. It was only later when he drove her back to her hotel that he remembered.

Good thing, too. The memory came just in the nick of time to prevent him from trying to sweep Chrissie into his arms again. He felt dangerously close to repeating the mistake he'd made the first night she was here.

She's only a client. Drew kept reminding himself. A client, moreover, who would most likely be returning to her established way of life in New Orleans. It made no sense to let his heart get involved.

But when he returned to his car after bidding a perfectly innocent good-night to Chrissie, there was no pride in his self-discipline. There was only a lot of simmering frustration.

Chapter Six

Chrissie inhaled deeply and paused for a long moment with her hand on the doorknob, gathering courage before she finally opened the door and went inside Laura's bedroom. The room was semidark and oppressive due to the gloomy rainy morning, but she did not immediately switch on a light. She went straight to the window and looked out at the rain-soaked patio and garden below.

She wished she wasn't here; she longed to be back home in her unpretentious apartment in New Orleans. She didn't want to sort through Laura Douglas's things; she didn't want to be in California one minute more.

Most of all, she didn't want these ambivalent feelings she had about Drew Casey.

She had neither seen nor heard from him since Friday evening when he'd taken her to dinner with his family. It was now Monday. Chrissie sighed as she watched the raindrops fall on the leaves of a eucalyptus tree. It shouldn't have bothered her that she hadn't heard from him; she shouldn't have expected it, much less hoped for it.

Chrissie caught her lower lip between her teeth and tried to will away the hurt she felt. She had no business aching from a sense of rejection. Drew had only been following orders by being kind enough to share that evening with her after her prearranged plans with Bob Raleigh had fallen through. There'd been nothing personal about it, and to think otherwise was only foolish self-deception.

Yet she couldn't seem to get the upper hand over her emotions. He'd been so warm and friendly that night, and his family had included her within their ranks as though she were someone special in Drew's life. The way he'd looked at her that evening had caused her to dare to believe she really did mean something to him. She still tingled as she recalled the way his eyes had softened when he'd watched her telling the story to his niece and nephew; she still experienced a stirring thrill over the warm, intimate way he'd smiled at her. There'd been something about his manner the entire evening that had led her to hope Drew was as drawn to her as she was to him. To her chagrin she'd even eagerly anticipated the moment when they would be alone, saying goodnight. She had been convinced that he would kiss her again as he had the first night. Worse, she had longed for it to happen.

When it hadn't, she'd felt flat, let down and pathetically disappointed. She'd gone into her lonely hotel room and glared with anger at her reflection in the mirror, wondering what was wrong with her, wondering what she had done to cause him to lose his former interest in her. Because the night he had kissed her, he had definitely been interested.

She was still no closer to an answer than she'd been on Friday night, and Chrissie was annoyed and impatient with herself for caring. The nicest favor she could do for herself would be to put Drew out of her mind altogether. If a man wasn't interested, it was sheer stupidity for a woman to keep weaving impossible dreams about him. Surely she had more pride than that!

At least, she told herself ruefully, now she knew for sure that Drew wasn't interested in her for her inheritance! But somehow that thought brought cold comfort.

She turned abruptly from the window, switched on a lamp and allowed her gaze to sweep the opulent bedroom. The day Jane White had shown her around, she'd beat a hasty retreat from this room without really examining anything. Now she was here to begin going through Laura's clothes and personal effects, and she didn't know where to start.

There were a number of objects on the dressing table— photographs, a jewelry box, crystal perfume bottles. Chrissie moved across the room, tentatively picked up one of the bottles of perfume and opened it. The scent was far too heavy for her own personal taste, and yet it was alluring and provocative. The exotic fragrance was at once a vivid, powerful statement about Laura Douglas as a flesh-and-blood person, not just a face on a movie screen.

Chrissie was about to open the jewelry box when the cluster of several photographs caught her attention instead. She bent closer for a better look, and all at once her mouth went dry. There was a portrait of a man of about fifty, whom she assumed was Martin Timms, Laura's husband; there was another photo of Laura and the same man laughing, squinting against the sun as they stood on a sailboat; but it was the third photograph that jolted her. It was a photograph of herself in cap and gown, taken on the day she'd graduated from L.S.U.

She shouldn't have been surprised. Hadn't her mother told her that she'd exchanged letters with Laura and sent her photographs? Still it was unexpected and jarring to find a familiar image of herself in an elegant sterling silver heart-shaped frame on the dressing table in the bedroom of the famous movie queen, Laura Douglas.

Chrissie turned her back on the photographs and went to the closet. It was as large as a small bedroom and her breath caught at the sight of so many beautiful clothes. For a long time she merely gazed at them in wonder, unwilling to touch anything. She had no idea where to begin sorting or what to do with the clothes. Certainly she wanted to keep none of them for herself.

On shelves in the back of the closet were a number of large boxes, each clearly labeled for contents. There were several containing fan mail, a couple containing publicity photographs and one for old magazines Laura had apparently liked to collect. Another was for mementos from travel.

There was one large metal file box without any labeling, and thinking it might contain important business papers of some sort, Chrissie picked it up and carried it into the bedroom. She sat down on the bed and opened it. When she did, she received a surprise that surpassed finding her own photograph on the dresser.

Inside the box was a packet of letters and a large leather-bound scrapbook. Chrissie picked up the stack of letters first and immediately recognized the handwriting on the top envelope as belonging to Marie. Quickly she thumbed through the rest and they were all addressed in that same familiar script. They were the letters Marie Barrows had written to Laura Douglas through the years. Laura, too, had apparently saved all Marie's communications just as Marie had done with Laura's letters.

Chrissie didn't open them. Instead she lifted the scrapbook out of the box and opened it. When she did, she caught her breath and felt sudden tears choking her throat.

There was a title page in the front of the scrapbook, and in beautiful script were the words, "My darling children."

With a trembling hand, Chrissie turned the page. The second page was filled with snapshots of two babies, identical twins who could be no other than herself and her sister, Victoria. Chrissie gazed at them for a long time. But on the following page were photographs of only one baby—herself. These were pictures she recognized just as she had the one on the dresser. Her parents had an album filled with these same photographs. In the margins Laura had written, "Chrissie at age ten months," or "Chrissie at her first Christmas."

The subsequent pages were devoted to a photographic chronicle of Chrissie's entire life. Besides copies of seemingly every photograph her parents had ever taken of her, there were many other little symbols of her growing years. There was an impression of a handprint that had been made in finger paints when she was three, a copy of an invitation to her fifth birthday party. There was a snip of pink fabric from the ballet costume her mother had made for her when she was seven. There was a picture of a clown she'd drawn when she was eight. There were newspaper clippings of sports columns in which her name had appeared when she'd played basketball in high school.

Chrissie closed the scrapbook, laid it beside her on the bed and for the first time she cried over the death of the mother she'd never known—the mother she'd been so determined to hate.

It was some time before the tears subsided, but when they did, Chrissie felt purged of a lifetime of resentment toward a mother she had believed didn't love her. Now she knew differently. A woman who didn't care wouldn't have meticulously kept a scrapbook that spanned the entire scope of her child's life. In Victoria's case, it hadn't been possible, so apparently Laura had focused all her secret longing on Chrissie.

Yet there were still many unanswered questions—the whys of parting the twins, of losing all contact with Victoria, of their father losing all claim to Christina. Sadly Chrissie realized the questions might never be answered. Yet at least in Laura's case Chrissie could now accept the knowledge that her birth mother had indeed loved her. True, she had given her up for adoption and never made any attempt to contact her, but these letters, photographs and mementos were clear evidence of a love Laura must have kept deeply buried inside her all those years.

For the first time, Chrissie was able to look at the situation from Laura's perspective. She had been spectacularly beautiful, a celebrated actress with all the trappings of fame and success. She'd had a wonderful career, the adoration of millions of moviegoers, apparently a loving as well as wealthy husband, this elegant fairy-tale mansion and more money than she could possibly spend. She'd seemed to have it all, the sort of life that many people envy and yearn to achieve, and yet all this time she had suffered her own private tragedy, no doubt filled with regrets and guilt over the alienation of both her children. Chrissie wondered what it must have been like for Laura, being denied one of the most treasured aspects of life for most women, that of being a mother. What had it been like to live amidst all the outward symbols of fame, glamour and splendor, knowing you couldn't touch your own children or watch them grow or ever be there for them when they needed the security and love that only a parent can give?

Sighing, Chrissie replaced the scrapbook inside the box with the letters, returned it to the closet and left the room.

Downstairs she found Jane White in the library, surrounded by a small mountain of business papers, tax returns and receipts.

"How're you coming along with your sorting?" Jane asked when Chrissie entered the room.

Chrissie sat down, sighed heavily and said, "I've accomplished nothing . . . and yet again . . . everything."

Jane lifted her eyebrows. "Come again?"

"I found a box with letters to Laura from my mother. There's also a scrapbook with pictures and mementos of my life. I realize now that Laura must have loved me in her own way."

"And how does that make you feel?" Jane asked curiously.

"Free, oddly enough."

"You resented her," Jane said.

"Actually I hated her. I hadn't realized just how intense that feeling was until it left me. I'd always felt she couldn't have cared or she wouldn't have given me away." Chrissie paused and sighed more softly. "I'm not sure if what I feel right now toward her memory is love, but at least it isn't hate anymore. Mostly I just feel pity. I don't think Laura could have been a happy woman, in spite of everything she had going for her."

"She wasn't," Jane replied. "Oh, I don't think she was actively miserable, exactly, but I never got the feeling that she was ever impressed with her looks and celebrity status or that her wealthy life-style particularly satisfied her. She was restless, always wanting to be doing something or going someplace, as though some inner demon wouldn't give her any peace. I never understood why, but then, of course, I didn't know about you and your sister. Maybe Laura was trying to run away from herself, from her thoughts and her painful memories."

"There's a photograph of me in her bedroom. Hadn't you ever seen it and wondered who it was?" Chrissie asked.

"Sure. Once I asked about it. Laura told me you were the daughter of a very old friend from her youth and that she loved you as she would her own daughter. In retrospect, I suppose that was as close to the truth as she could bring herself to get.''

They were interrupted by the maid who appeared in the doorway and announced, ''Mr. Casey is here to see Miss Barrows.''

Jane rose from behind the desk. ''Show him in, Betsy.'' To Chrissie, she added, ''I'll make myself scarce and see how Alice is coming along with lunch. Do you want me to have Betsy serve coffee while Mr. Casey is here?''

''That sounds like a good idea. Thanks.''

Chrissie had tensed at the mention of Drew's name. She got to her feet, unconsciously patted her hair and wondered why he had come.

A moment later Drew strode energetically into the room. At once the atmosphere seemed charged with a vitality it had previously lacked. As usual on working days, he was dressed in a conservative suit, this time a dark blue, and she had time to think that somehow he was able to transform ordinary business clothes into a look that was extraordinarily attractive. Maybe it was the subtle power of his shoulders filling out the jacket, or the way the slacks accentuated his long, slim but well-muscled legs. For many men, suits concealed a multitude of physical imperfections; on Drew they simply enhanced his superb physique.

With a shock, Chrissie realized she was concentrating on Drew's body in an intensely personal way. She was burningly aware of him, and she resented this unreasonable disturbance of her emotions.

It would never do to let him know how much she'd missed him these past two days, or how affected she was by his presence now. Gathering the remnants of her self-control, she raised her eyes to his face and spoke in a deliberately unruffled tone. ''This is a surprise. How did you know where to find me?''

"You weren't at the hotel, so I took a chance you'd be here."

"I suppose you've come to discuss more of those dreary old business matters."

Drew nodded. "I guess you could say that."

Chrissie was crestfallen. Deep inside, contrary to logic, she'd hoped he had come to see her because he *wanted* to see her. It just went to show how pathetic she was.

"I see." Her voice was lackluster and subdued. "Have a seat, then. We may as well get it over with."

Drew struggled to maintain a poker face. "You know," he said, "this is really a nice house. It's a terrific place for entertaining."

Chrissie stared at him blankly. What did that have to do with anything? she wondered.

"So?"

"So...I was thinking maybe it's about time you gave a party. A week from Sunday would be a good time for one, don't you think?"

"A party?" Chrissie asked in astonishment. The last thing on her mind these days were parties. "Why would I want to do that? I don't even know anybody in L.A. except for the people at the law firm and your family." Her eyes narrowed suspiciously. She was pretty sure Drew was teasing her, but to what end she couldn't imagine. "And anyway, why a week from Sunday in particular? Is that your birthday or something?"

"If it was, would you throw me a party?" he countered.

Drew's eyes were definitely twinkling. Chrissie sighed with exasperation and said shortly, "I'm more liable to throw something *at* you if you don't start talking plain sense. I have no intention of throwing a party for anyone, and especially not in this house! I haven't even worked up the nerve to spend a night here yet."

Drew grinned broadly and fastened his gaze on Chrissie's face. Not for the world would he miss her first reaction to what he was about to say.

"Well," he drawled, "I just thought you might like to give a rousing welcome to your twin sister on her first evening in the good old U.S. of A., but of course if you're dead set against the notion, we'll just forget abo—"

"You've found her!" Chrissie shrieked.

Drew half chuckled, half groaned as the breath was practically knocked out of him. In her excitement, Chrissie had hurled herself right smack into him.

Drew wrapped his arms around her waist, pinning her close as her arms curled around his neck. He chuckled once more, delighted over her delight, and then he did what any normal man with such an armful of loveliness and uninhibited joy would do. He kissed her thoroughly and soundly, and to hell with the consequences.

Over the weekend, he'd fought like the dickens against his desire to see her, and it hadn't been easy. She'd been so much fun Friday evening, fitting right in with his family as though she belonged there and being so darned attractive and appealing that it had conjured up all sorts of futile yearnings in him. It had been impossibly difficult to part with her at her hotel room door without kissing her when she'd looked so enticingly kissable, but he'd managed it. On Saturday and Sunday he'd stayed as busy as possible, working out his frustrations at the gym, on the tennis court, jogging, and sailing to Catalina Island with a buddy on his sailboat.

Yet none of his feverish activities had been able to completely stamp out his confusing feelings for Chrissie, and this morning when he'd gotten the transatlantic call from London, he'd felt a quickening thrill because it meant he had a perfectly legitimate excuse to seek her out again. And quite simply he'd wanted to be the one to share her elation when she learned her sister had been located. If anyone had challenged his right to impart the news, he'd have fought them—even Raleigh himself.

Fortunately that hadn't been necessary and meanwhile, as he held her, Drew was far from averse to the present situation. To be honest with himself, it was entirely to his liking.

He kissed Chrissie over and over again. Her body was warm and soft, trembling with excitement. How much of the trembling was due to the news or the effect of his kisses, he couldn't tell. But one thing he knew. She wasn't fighting him.

Quite the contrary. And that suited him just fine, too. Chrissie was burrowed up to him, and her pale blue top seemed like next to nothing between her lush, full breasts and his chest. Her snug-fitting white slacks lay smoothly over her trim, curving hips where his fingers rested lightly just below the waist. As for her lips... they were warm and pliable and sweet and Drew was absolutely convinced he'd never tasted anything more potent in his life.

Drew became aware of the heat surging through his body, of his heart racing. He was fast losing all control, and he didn't even care. All he cared about was how desperately he wanted her—all of her.

At last he dragged his lips from her mouth and pressed his face against her cheek as he inhaled oxygen deep into his lungs. A tremor shook him, and he whispered raggedly, "Chrissie..."

At that precise moment the door opened. Both of them heard the sound of it. Instantly Drew felt Chrissie tense, and then with haste she disentangled herself from his embrace and turned.

"I...I'm so sorry, ma'am," mumbled the woman who had entered. "Miss White sent me to bring coffee."

"Yes...that's right. Just...set it on the table, Betsy. Thank you."

Chrissie's voice, though slightly breathless, was remarkably stable under the circumstances. Personally Drew was glad he wasn't called upon to speak at the moment. He was having a devil of a time beating down the flames of passion that still simmered his blood.

It seemed an eternity before the maid withdrew and closed the door, but of course it had been only moments. By then Drew more or less had himself under control, which was essential since he had a pretty strong hunch that Chrissie wasn't going to fling herself into his arms again. She hadn't looked at him once since Betsy's arrival. She had carefully kept her back to him, and it was stiff and straight.

Even when they were alone again, Chrissie didn't turn around or speak. Drew waited and waited, but nothing happened. At last he asked humorously, "Aren't you ever going to look at me again?"

In a flash, she turned. Chrissie's face was pink with embarrassment, and her eyes were bright with emotion. "It's not funny!" she snapped heatedly.

At once Drew was somber. "Am I laughing?"

Chrissie nibbled at her lip and after a long time raised her gaze to his face. "I shouldn't have...I'm sorry I...I threw myself at you that way. Please forgive me."

Drew's amusement returned full force. He couldn't resist grinning before he demanded, "You don't actually expect me to pretend I *minded*, do you?"

Chrissie's blush deepened. She was charmingly flustered, and Drew was genuinely amazed at the extent of her embarrassment. Was it because of what happened between them, or because her exuberant impulse had been the catalyst? Or was it that she regretted the whole thing altogether?

Suddenly he had to know. It seemed vitally urgent. Drew went to her, cupped her face between his hands and said softly, "I enjoyed every single kiss we just shared. Are you sorry we got caught at it like a couple of teenagers in the back seat of an old Chevy, or are you sorry because it happened?"

Chrissie had no idea what to answer until she saw once again the telltale twinkle in his eyes. "Damn it, Andrew Casey, it was embarrassing getting caught!"

"Is that all?"

She could no longer meet his eyes. "You know it's not. I'm ashamed of the way I went at you and... well, sort of pressured you."

"Hmm. Yes, I am feeling browbeaten and pressured and sort of wimpy." Chrissie giggled and met his eyes again. Drew nodded in satisfaction. "That's better. Now tell me this... would it have bothered you if I'd made the first move?"

Chrissie felt her cheeks grow warmer, but this time she forced herself to keep eye contact. "No," she answered truthfully.

"So... it wasn't my kisses that bothered you?"

"No."

"That's good enough for me. What we have here is sexism on your part, Chrissie. You women cry equality to high heavens, yet here you are wanting the man to make all the aggressive moves because that way you don't have to face the threat of rejection. Well, we guys are just as susceptible to that feeling ourselves. I wanted to kiss you when I took you home from Mom's dinner, but I was afraid you'd react like you did the first night. I didn't want to be rejected, either."

Chrissie gazed at him in astonishment and expanding happiness. "Is that true?"

"Sure, it's true. So personally I think what just went on in here was the ice breaker we both needed."

Chrissie's heart was thudding so loudly, she was afraid he might hear it. She loved the soft melting expression in Drew's eyes as his hand still cradled her face. She wanted to speak, but she couldn't think of a word. She was a mass of feelings—happy, hopeful feelings.

Drew seemed to sense that the subject had gone far enough for now. He smiled, dropped his hands from her cheeks and prosaically suggested, "Maybe we ought to have that coffee while it's still hot."

Relief surged through Chrissie. She needed a respite from her turbulent emotions. Besides, her mind swirled with questions about her sister. All she knew so far was that Victoria had been located and would arrive a week from Sunday.

She managed to pour their coffee into cups without spilling it, though her hand was still slightly unsteady.

"Tell me about Victoria," she said when she handed Drew his cup. "Where is she? When did you find out about her?"

She took a seat on the sofa a safe distance away from the chair he had taken. It was just as well, Drew thought. They could both use a little perspective after those high-voltage kisses.

"Bill Chamberlain called an hour ago. He found Victoria, and wanted you to get the news as soon as possible." His mouth stretched into a smile. "Bill said she was quite excited to learn about you. He also passed along word that if you'll be at your hotel at four o'clock this afternoon, Victoria will telephone you."

Chrissie's eyes lit up. "I'll be there!" she exclaimed with deep feeling. "I wouldn't miss that call for anything!"

"I figured as much," Drew said with a grin. His gaze and voice softened. "I'm happy for you, Chrissie. Really happy."

"Thanks." Her voice was husky. "I'm happy for me, too. It's a dream come true." She sipped at her coffee and was silent for a while. Then she asked, "Does she live in London? Is that where Bill Chamberlain found her?"

"Yes. She lives in a flat in a modest section of London with her husband. Bill finally tracked her down by checking marriage records."

"Married." Chrissie mused over the words. Oddly that possibility hadn't crossed her mind before. "Does she also have children?"

"Bill didn't mention any, so I think not. Of course you'll be able to find that out later when you speak with her. Her married name is Nash," Drew went on. "I understand she works in the business office of a hotel in Knightsbridge. Her husband, Paul, is a professional photographer. He'll be accompanying her to California."

"Wonderful." Chrissie quietly digested the few facts Drew had told her. It was very little, but already it made Victoria seem like a real flesh-and-blood person instead of a mere figment of her own mind.

Suddenly she smiled. "You were right to think of a party. Drew. Of course I must have a party in their honor! I can hardly wait! I'll invite everyone at the law firm, and perhaps the management firm, as well. And do you suppose your family would like to come?"

"I'm sure they would very much enjoy meeting your sister, Chrissie, but if you're just thinking you should repay a dinner debt, forget it. Including my family on your guest list isn't necessary."

"But I want to!" she insisted. "I liked them tremendously. Except for the business people I've met, they're the only people I'm acquainted with in this city. It would please me a great deal if they would come and help welcome my twin."

Drew nodded. "Then I'll pass along your invitation. I'm sure they'll be delighted." He finished his coffee, and when he set his cup on the table next to him, his gaze fell on the desk with its clutter of papers and folders. "Are you making headway in sorting through Laura's things?"

Chrissie sighed. "It's more difficult than I'd expected. There are so many business papers and pieces of correspondence. Jane's been going through the files and throwing out everything that can be discarded, but I'll have to study the remainder. A lot of it concerns current business. Then there're the clothes and household items, not to mention the jewelry at the bank. Yesterday Betsy and I packed up some clothes to give to charity, but I'm at a standstill about what to do with most of Laura's things. The furnishings and art works will have to be appraised, of course, before anything can be done with them."

"When Victoria arrives, it ought to be easier," Drew said. "You'll be able to decide together what each of you wants to keep and what should be sold or auctioned."

Chrissie nodded. "It'll be a relief to share the decision-making. Of course I have no idea how Victoria will feel, but if I have my way, everything will be liquidated and the proceeds divided right down the middle. That way Victoria can take her half of the money and do whatever she wants with it, and so can I. Without the burden of all these properties, I can give my share to charity and be done with the whole ordeal."

Drew was appalled and asked incredulously, "You want to give it all away?"

"Well, most of it." Chrissie shrugged. "I don't feel comfortable about accepting all that money, and I certainly don't feel comfortable with the burden of it. All I want is to be out from under all these obligations and get my life back to normal."

"That's the most cowardly, irresponsible attitude I ever heard!" Drew hunched forward, hands clasped over one knee, and he gave her a stern, hard look. "It might be admirable to desire to help charities, Chrissie, but for God's sake, think about what you're planning to do before you get rid of all the money in one lump sum! You'll be abdicating your responsibility and placing the power of that money in the hands of a stranger... whoever happens to be in the driver's seat of the charity organization you choose to give it to. How do you know that person will use the money wisely? Far too many people have fallen prey to their own greed when they're given access to unlimited, unprotected funds! Think about this! You could do a whole lot more good for other people in the long run if you bothered to learn how to manage that money yourself, continue to increase it and judiciously distribute portions of it to various charities as you see a need."

"But that's just it!" Chrissie exclaimed. "I don't want to do all that! Don't you see? It scares me. I'm a schoolteacher, not a financial expert! It makes me nervous having other people dependent on me for their living. As it is, there's the household staff here, the managers of the farm and ranch and all those other holdings. I feel like the whole world's come crashing down on my shoulders and I'm supposed to take care of all these people somehow! It's not fair! It's not my money in the first place!"

"It won't be as bad as you think," Drew pointed out reasonably. "The management firm handles most of the load already as it is. And you know that any of us at the law firm are willing to assist you with problems or questions. All I'm saying is to give yourself a little time to get used to it. Once you get familiar with all the facets of the business interests, you'll start to feel more comfortable and confident. If you do something hasty like getting rid of everything at once, you'll regret it for a long, long time."

Drew's criticism stung her. Somewhere deep inside her, Chrissie knew everything he was saying was right, but she didn't want to hear it. She didn't want criticism or advice. She wanted only understanding, and that, Drew refused to give her. Angrily she demanded, "What difference does it make to you what I do with my share of the inheritance? It's not your money, after all! I guess I can do as I darn well please!"

"Sure you can!" Drew was angry now, too. He got to his feet, and his face was stony as he glared down at her. "You've got a perfect right to toss every last dollar into a trash can if that's what you want to do! But as your attorney, it's my job to advise you, and I hate to see you foolishly throw everything away. If Laura Douglas had wanted her entire estate to be given to charity, without responsible supervision by somebody she cared about, don't you suppose she would have made arrangements to dispose of it that way herself? It seems to me you owe your own mother's memory enough respect to see that her legacy isn't stupidly wasted or squandered."

Chrissie was on her feet now, too, and she was trembling with rage. "Who are you to judge me about what I owe to Laura Douglas's memory? I'm the kid she gave away, remember? I have a really hard time seeing anything worthy of respect in that, and just because she happened to leave me a large sum of money doesn't change a thing! I don't owe her anything!"

Drew's voice was deep and controlled. "I can see there's no reasoning with you while you're in this mood, so perhaps it's best if I leave now. When you come to your senses, you know where to reach me."

After Drew was gone, Chrissie dissolved into tears. She slumped on the sofa and sobbed with anger, grief and pain. Upstairs, when she'd found the scrapbook, she'd felt a softening toward Laura. But just now she'd belligerently challenged Drew's suggestion that she owed her mother's memory any respect.

She was so confused, so tired and so intimidated by all these sudden, overwhelming changes. Nothing was the same as it had once been. Nothing was simple anymore.

And not least of her disturbed emotions were her feelings about Drew. His judgmental condemnation of her character had wounded her deeply. Earlier he had kissed her with such passion that it had shaken her to her very soul, convincing her that he really cared for her. But if he believed she was such a terrible person because she felt no sense of obligation toward the memory of a mother who had never been a mother, obviously the only thing he had felt toward her had been mere physical attraction and nothing more. That thought only increased her anguish.

The question of why it should matter so much what Drew thought of her tormented her, but she was afraid of the answer. Somehow Chrissie knew that the answer would be more seriously disturbing than anything that had gone before, and just now she simply couldn't cope with it.

Resolutely, she dried her eyes. There was still much to be done. She got to her feet and went in search of the secretary. There was a party to be planned and bedrooms to be prepared. She would, she decided, move into the house tonight. Maybe she wasn't willing to take control of everything that had been Laura's, but she could, and would, take charge of the household for the time being.

Chapter Seven

John Keene and Drew were sharing a drink in a bar a block away from their office. A short time before, a meeting with the senior partners of the firm concerning the assignment of new cases had ended. It was now almost five o'clock in the afternoon, and the two men were rehashing the developments of the meeting.

John's new assignment was a civil suit concerning a dispute between two business partners. Drew's was infinitely more juicy—he would be handling a criminal defense case involving a client accused of running a large-scale smuggling operation from Colombia. What made it really interesting was that the man, Kevin Wellington, was the son of a highly respected Los Angeles businessman and philanthropist with political connections some said even led as far as the White House. The elder Wellington was also a close personal friend of George Pitts, one of the law firm's retired partners. Naturally Drew was elated. All along he had wanted to specialize in criminal cases, and to be trusted with such an important case was a powerful statement of the partners' faith in his abilities.

"You lucky dog!" John lifted his glass of Scotch in a salute to Drew. "I'd give a lot to be able to sink my teeth into a case like yours."

Drew grinned. "If you expect me to feel sorry for you, pal, forget it! I can hardly believe my own good fortune. And anyway, this sort of case isn't up your alley."

"I know. I'm pegged as a dollars-and-cents detail man, and I'm not really complaining. I'm good at wading through financial records and getting at the truth, and I enjoy it, but somehow my kind of work just doesn't have the same kind of pizzazz as the Wellington case. More power to you, Casey."

"Thanks." Drew took a sip of his drink, then said with all seriousness, "Now all I have to do is pull it off."

"I've watched you, Drew," John said thoughtfully. "You're a good team player. When you were given boring, routine assignments, you did your job with meticulous care. You're thorough, and you've got a golden tongue when you speak in a courtroom. This is going to be a tough, possibly sensational trial, and the partners wanted the best man for the job. You're that man."

"Well . . . thanks." John's words were heartening. All the same, Drew didn't permit himself the indulgence of basking in their glow. This case was going to involve a tremendous amount of hard work, consume all his energy and extract every ounce of intelligence and ability he possessed. He welcomed the challenge, but he was realistic about the chances of a successful outcome. The district attorney was not going to hand it to him without a tough fight.

For the next half hour the two men talked shop, sports and vacations. Next month John and his wife, Janet, would be traveling to Hawaii. Drew hadn't yet scheduled his vacation time, nor did he have any particular desire to go away, but John thought he should do so soon.

"You'd better get your vacation over with before you sink knee-deep in this Wellington thing. When that happens, it might be months before you have any spare time."

Drew shrugged. "I'll wait. I don't have anything special planned, and I can't see hanging around my apartment for two weeks being bored to death. I'd rather work."

"You need a wife," John teased. "They make you take time to relax whether you like it or not."

Drew grinned. "Maybe you're right. But a man can't exactly get a wife as easily as picking up a gallon of milk at the supermarket, you know."

John chuckled. "Think how much trouble a fellow could save himself if he could." Humorously he intoned, "I'll take one in blond, please... beautiful, sexy, a terrific lover, thrifty, an excellent mother and housekeeper with a perpetually sunny disposition, who will spoil me shamelessly." He polished off his drink and stood up. "Too bad, but I guess you'll just have to do it the hard way like the rest of us. Meantime I'd better head home. Janet, who *doesn't* spoil me, expects me to help her do some yard work before it gets dark."

Drew laughed and got to his feet, too. When they left the bar, they walked together back to the parking garage where they parted to go their separate ways.

Drew didn't want to go home to his empty apartment. He was restless, keyed up, churning with unleashed energy.

He was also... longing to see Chrissie.

It had been two days since he'd seen her. They hadn't parted on the most cordial of terms. She'd been adamant about getting rid of her legacy and the responsibility that went with it; he of course had been dead set against such a rash, foolish course of action. Probably she still had her head set about it. Certainly he hadn't changed his opinion.

But all that aside, he wanted to see her again, and his desire had nothing to do with business.

Drew supposed he should have told John of Chrissie's intentions, since it was John who handled the complex details concerning Laura Douglas's finances. Drew's task had been to locate the twins and inform them in a broad way about their inheritance. In essence his job was practically over. John would be as appalled as Drew when he heard what Chrissie was thinking of doing, but Drew was hoping that it wouldn't actually come to that. Optimistically he was banking on Victoria's influence once she arrived. Surely she would be saner about the subject of the money than Chrissie was at the moment and would be able to convince her twin not to be foolhardy.

Drew stopped at a red light. It was funny, he thought to himself, that John should have brought up the subject of a wife for him. For the past two days, after he'd cooled off about Chrissie's ridiculous attitude toward her inheritance, the stark truth had shone through all else. He was in love with her—deeply, unequivocally, madly in love—and he was still trying to come to terms with it.

When viewed dispassionately, it simply wasn't possible. He'd been acquainted with Chrissie for such a short time, so how well could he really know her? It hadn't been very long ago when he'd thought he loved Carol, so the past couple of days he'd made himself closely examine his feelings toward Chrissie to be certain that it wasn't mere infatuation.

It wasn't. He'd finally had to conclude that the feelings were real indeed. Drew had never felt this strongly about Carol. There was something about Chrissie that touched him on a deep level. She was beautiful all right, vivacious, charming, and he ached right down to his bones to be able to make love to her. His nights were tortured with fantasies about holding her in his arms, with their bodies pressed together in the heat of a mutual passion. But as much as he yearned for her physically, the way he felt about Chrissie went deeper than sexual attraction. He found himself wanting her happiness and well-being above his own; he discovered that of all things, he wanted nothing to ever hurt her again as she'd been hurt by a mother who had given her away. Nor did he want her to hurt herself, which he was certain she would do if she really did give up all the power and responsibility that went with possessing her share of her mother's estate. He wanted to be the man to take care of her through good times and bad. He wanted her smiles, her laughter, her tears and sorrows, and he wanted to have the right to lavish his love and support upon her through it all. He wanted to be her best friend, as well as her lover, and he wanted all those same things from her in return. In short, Drew wanted all of her, heart and mind, her body, her children, her constant presence in his days and in his nights, and he wanted to give her equally of himself.

The intensity of all those emotions had allowed him no peace. The past two nights he'd had trouble falling asleep; during the day, he'd had to exert a fierce self-discipline just to pay attention to his work.

His feelings about Chrissie, and now the fresh excitement over getting the plum Wellington case, all combined to set his energies boiling. Drew desperately needed to work out the pressures, to find a physical outlet for the cauldron of emotions trapped and steaming in his body.

He could go to the gym, of course, but that notion wasn't appealing. That wouldn't solve anything except perhaps to serve as a temporary physical release. Mentally and emotionally he'd still be in a turmoil.

Drew was suddenly tired of fighting himself. It was a futile ordeal.

When he reached the next red light, he changed directions, heading purposefully in the direction of Bel Air.

* * *

In the Early American bedroom at the mansion, which Chrissie was now using as her own, she stripped off her clothes and pulled on the black-and-gold bikini she'd bought yesterday in a boutique on Rodeo Drive. She still felt slightly sinful for having parted with so much money for it, but turning to the mirror, she told her reflection that she'd earned it. All day today she and Jane had worked hard, plowing through a mountain of papers in the library, and now she felt drained. Jane had left only fifteen minutes before and Chrissie impulsively decided to take a swim. She needed physical activity after hours of mental strain while sitting cramped in a chair.

It was the housekeeper's day off, and Chrissie was pleased to have an evening of solitude stretching before her. This was the first time since coming to Los Angeles that she'd been completely on her own. Fine hotel service and having a full-time housekeeper and cook here at the mansion were all well and good, but she had been accustomed to taking care of her own needs and she rather looked forward to fending for herself tonight. After her dip in the pool she would raid the refrigerator for cold cuts or go out for a hamburger. She might even pick up a paperback to read later in bed.

From the adjoining bathroom, Chrissie grabbed a thick towel before she left the bedroom and went down the hall. As she passed the Mexican bedroom, however, she paused, opened the door and stepped inside. It was the room she and Alice had chosen for Vicky and Paul to occupy when they arrived. The room was vivid with splashes of bright colors contrasting with somber dark wood. A silver-trimmed black sombrero hung on a wall, and a striped serape was draped across the foot of the bed. At Chrissie's request the gardener had brought up several plants from the patio to provide living greenery. In one corner was a fan-shaped tropical plant; in another was a bamboo palm. On the window ledge and dresser were flowering begonias and crimson geraniums in clay pots. Chrissie hadn't seen the room since the plants had been brought in, and now she was satisfied that the room was both welcoming and inviting.

It seemed as though the day of Vicky's arrival would never come, and eager impatience boiled in Chrissie's veins. Waiting for Christmas morning to arrive had never been so difficult as this!

When Vicky had telephoned her two days ago, they had talked for an incredible three hours! Chrissie grinned with pleasure at the memory, stepped back into the hallway and pulled the bedroom door shut. She and Vicky had alternately laughed and cried and laughed again, and had told each other pertinent facts about their lives. They'd been amazed and thrilled to learn that each of them loved gardening and plants, that both of them liked classical as well as rock music, that blue was the favorite color of each and that both of them were allergic to chocolate. There had been many other similarities, as well, and no doubt they would discover even more once they were together.

But that was still a week and a half away. When they'd finally hung up, Chrissie had promised to telephone Vicky early next week so that they could talk again. Neither of them was willing to wait until Vicky's arrival in the United States to talk again now that they had found each other. Chrissie felt a lovely warmth surrounding her heart each time she thought of her sister. Just speaking on the phone had established a closeness between them that promised a lifetime bond nothing would ever break. Hearing her twin's voice and anticipating soon being with her in person was the most wonderful thing that had ever happened in Chrissie's entire life.

It was also the only happiness she had at the moment. Though Chrissie had settled into the mansion, it could never feel like home. She didn't belong in this elegant milieu. It made her uncomfortable, and the sooner she was done with it all and could go back home, the better.

That thought brought a quick frown as it reminded her of the sharp disagreement with Drew. He contended that she would be doing a terrible disservice to Laura's memory if she gave away her inheritance, and he thought she wanted to do it out of resentment toward her mother. But it wasn't like that. Chrissie believed she'd come to terms with her feelings concerning her mother. No, it was the sheer magnitude of so much money, so much property and so many possessions, so many other people depending on that wealth for their livelihoods, and the great burden of responsibility that intimidated her. She understood nothing about investments, running businesses, tax write-offs or dealing as an authority over employees, and she didn't want to learn. It seemed to Chrissie that a person needed to be hard-boiled and shrewd to control that much money and exert that much power, and she didn't have either the personality or the training for the job. What she planned to do was to be generous in terminating Laura's household employees and the managers of the farms and estates, and she would give the management firms plenty of notice so they could replace her business with new clients. For herself, she would tuck away some of that money to cover possible occasional trips to London and transatlantic phone calls. The bulk of her fortune would be distributed among several charities she favored. Otherwise the money simply threatened to complicate her life beyond her ability to cope.

But Drew neither understood her fears nor considered them important. His implacable attitude had hurt, particularly since it had followed those wild, thrilling kisses. She'd been so caught up in the flood of heated emotions the kisses had aroused in her, as well as floating high on the news that Vicky had been located, that when he'd later come down hard on her, her buoyant feelings had burst like a fragile soap bubble.

She hadn't talked with Drew since, and while she didn't like admitting it, she missed him. She missed his friendly teasing, the compassion he'd offered when she'd still been longing to learn the whereabouts of her twin, the matter-of-fact way he'd guided her through the complicated maze of business details. Most of all, she just plain missed him...his living, breathing, vital presence, his energy, his smile...his touch. Especially that.

Chrissie reached the bottom of the stairs and headed down the wide central hallway toward the back of the house. She had just reached the patio door when the front door-bell rang.

She paused and nibbled her lip in consternation. She hadn't bothered to wear a wrap over her bathing suit since she was alone in the house. Now someone was at the door, and here she stood wearing only a very skimpy bikini.

She wasn't expecting visitors. Only now did she remember that Jane had mentioned that the electronic security system that controlled the front gate was on the blink and had been disconnected until repairmen could come tomorrow. Anyone, literally anyone, could have driven through the gate unimpeded and could now be standing on the other side of the front door.

Chrissie considered ignoring the bell. The last thing she wanted was for a stranger to see her dressed in a revealing French bikini, especially not when she was alone in this vast house.

The bell rang again, more insistently. Sighing, Chrissie went toward the front door, draping her towel around her shoulders as she went.

There was a small peephole in the door, and prudently Chrissie stood on tiptoes to look through it. If the caller was a stranger, she would not open the door.

But she recognized the man standing there. It was Drew. Her heart began to thud erratically and her body registered a soaring rise in temperature. She was instantly, absurdly, insanely happy to see him.

But she hoped none of those reactions showed in her face as she pulled open the door a moment later. She carefully stood to one side of the door so that the lower half of her body was concealed as she peered around it.

"Hello." Her voice was soft—too soft, she realized nervously. Quickly masking her melting feminine delight at seeing Drew, she asked in a sturdier voice, "What brings you here?"

"You," Drew answered bluntly. "I wanted to see you. Is that okay?"

"I...suppose so." Chrissie caught her breath. There was an intensity in his gaze that was most disturbing, and his straightforward reply knocked her even more off balance.

A strained silence fell as they looked at each other. Finally Drew asked, "Are you going to invite me in, or did I come at a bad time?" His dark gaze took in the towel hanging around her neck. The rest of Chrissie was still out of sight behind the massive door. "Did I get you out of the shower or something?"

Chrissie shook her head and found her voice again. "No. I was just about to take a swim."

"Ah." Suddenly Drew's eyes were twinkling. "Then it's a bathing suit you're hiding behind this door."

"Well..."

Drew grinned. "My guess is a bikini." He closed his eyes. "Blue, with purple and orange flowers on it." He opened his eyes once more and demanded, "Let's see how accurate my psychic ability is."

"It's zero percent accurate," Chrissie assured him. Sudden amusement lurked in her eyes, but stubbornly she did not budge from her position behind the door.

"Prove it."

"Give me one good reason why I should," she challenged.

"I'm involved in this research project that deals with ESP and psychic phenomena concerning beautiful young ladies, you see. It's very important to document the results of all my efforts. I really must insist that I personally observe whether the bikini looks like the one I saw in my mind's eye. Strictly in the interests of science, you understand."

Chrissie laughed. Here once more was the Drew she was rapidly falling in love with—warm, humorous and fun loving. "In the interests of science, I guess I'll have to show you how off the mark you are, then, won't I?" Since she couldn't feasibly cower behind the door for the rest of her life, she stepped out into full view.

Drew's gaze abandoned her face and traveled very slowly downward. Chrissie could actually feel the impact of the burning gaze as it paused at strategic locations along her body. She sucked in a ragged breath.

Drew gave a low whistle. "Dynamite!" Their eyes met as he added, "I may've been wrong about the color, but I always knew that under your clothes there was a fantastic body. I was right about that!"

Chrissie's face warmed with pleasure, and the expression in his eyes was making her feel more breathless than ever. The situation was fast getting out of control. It was plainly up to her to pull in the reins. "Now that you know you were wrong about the color, I'll go change into something a bit more modest," she said primly. "You can wait in the library if you like."

"I'd rather go swimming with you," Drew told her.

Chrissie lifted her eyebrows and gave him what she hoped was a withering look. "And just what do you propose to wear? Your birthday suit?"

"Why not?" Drew countered with a wicked light in his eyes. "It's a private pool with a high fence around it. You could discard those absurdly tiny black-and-gold strips of cloth you optimistically call a bathing suit, and we could skinny-dip together. It could," he drawled, "be a whole lot of fun."

"Tempting as your suggestion is," Chrissie said dryly, "I think I'll pass. Skinny-dipping could create a dangerous situation."

Drew's grin widened. "I was pinning my hopes on just that."

"You're terrible!" Chrissie scolded. "Absolutely shameless!"

"Probably," Drew conceded. "But you'll have to admit I'm a man who recognizes a good opportunity when he sees it." Before Chrissie could retort, he added in a normal voice, "Seriously, I'd enjoy a swim myself. I could use the exercise. And strictly on the up-and-up, since you insist. I have a suit in the car."

"You carry it around with you?" Chrissie asked in surprise.

"Sure. I've got a duffel bag full of gym clothes. I work out at an athletic club a few times a week. I usually go straight from the office, so it's handier to keep them in the car."

"Hmm. All right, get them."

Chrissie watched as Drew ran down the steps toward his car. Suddenly the evening ahead looked exciting and fun.

While Drew changed in the bathroom just off the front hall, Chrissie went outside to the terrace. At poolside she slipped off her thongs, sat down and dangled her feet in the blue water. Without warning, one tumultuous thought tumbled over another, all of them having to do with Drew. His unexpected presence had unnerved her more than she'd thought. Chrissie's breath became quick and shallow.

What if they developed an intimate relationship? It was obvious enough that beneath all Drew's outrageous teasing, there had been a streak of seriousness. He wanted her sexually; just as plainly, she wanted him, too. It would be easy enough to yield to the insistent pressures of that attraction, but what about afterward? What about when the estate business was finally settled—when the hot summer days ended? Would he then try to stop her from returning to New Orleans and her life there? Would it even matter to him whether she went or stayed?

They'd known each other such a brief time . . . not even a month. Chrissie simply didn't know Drew well enough yet to be able to fully trust him. She had trusted the wrong man once, when she'd been engaged to Barry, and she'd known him for well over a year! By contrast she hardly knew Drew at all, and a cautious part of her mind told her to be careful, to be certain before she got too involved. Impulsiveness could lead too easily to a broken heart.

But all the warnings to herself were instantly forgotten when Drew emerged from the house. Chrissie's senses became acutely attuned to his blatant sexual magnetism.

A puff of breeze stirred his dark brown hair across his wide brow. His skin was a golden sun-touched color, enhancing his exquisite masculine build. His chest and shoulders were hardened muscles. Thick dark hair covered most of his chest, trailing off to nothing down the length of his tapered torso. Below his tan swimming trunks, his long legs boasted powerful thighs. The sheer size and rock-solid strength of his body testified to his superior athletic fitness. It was easy to understand why he'd once been a football player. Chrissie wondered fleetingly as he came toward her whether the cheerleaders had not been just a little bit in love with him. She was becoming more and more convinced that she was herself.

She promptly discarded that notion when he rudely shoved her into the pool. This was clearly war, and accordingly, Chrissie went into battle. She grabbed one of his feet and tugged, pitching Drew forward. There was a loud, probably painful, belly-busting splat.

For the next half hour, they played like frisky children. They dunked each other, raced and played catch with an inflated ball. It was precisely the sort of vigorous physical exertion Drew needed to work out the tension and frustration that had built up in him the past few days.

Chrissie's physical capacity for a lively workout matched Drew's. She might have been the sort to go for a couple of leisurely laps across the pool and call it a day, but instead she was as rough-and-tumble as any ten-year-old tomboy, giving as good as she got. Her playful spirit only made Drew more crazy about her.

When they were pleasantly exhausted and climbed out of the pool, Chrissie grabbed her towel, dabbed it to her arms and legs and asked, "How about a cold drink?"

"Sounds like a winner."

Drew dried off as Chrissie walked toward the house. He watched her go, thoroughly enjoying the sight of her glorious hips swaying gently as she walked.

When she had vanished inside the house, Drew flopped down on a cushioned chaise longue and sighed contentedly. The afternoon sun was beginning to disappear behind the screen of trees at the edge of the property, and the air was pleasantly cool on his damp skin.

Drew closed his eyes, not really thinking about anything. For the moment, he was happy with the breeze on his face and the knowledge that shortly Chrissie would be returning to his side. He needed nothing else.

He still didn't open his eyes when he heard the door slam and Chrissie's thongs flip-flop across the tiled terrace. When she reached his chair, he could feel her presence even before she spoke.

"Hey...lazy bones! You can't fall asleep now. I won't let you. You promised to take me out for a hamburger later, and I intend to hold you to it. Besides," she threatened ominously, "if you go to sleep, I'm going to pour this drink over your head, ice and all."

In a flash, Drew's eyes flew open and one hand went out to grasp her wrist. His fingers closed forcefully about her slender wrist, and he tugged her down until she had no recourse except to sit on the chaise beside him, at the same time precariously balancing the two iced drinks in her hands.

"Nobody," Drew gave a low growl, "but nobody, gets by threatening me with violence!"

Chrissie's blue eyes sparkled with swift delight. "Oh, no? And just how do you think you're going to stop me?"

Drew released her wrist and in one fluid motion removed the glasses from her hands, set them on the terrace beside the chair and wrapped his arms around her, drawing her down to lie nestled against his chest. "Like this," he answered. His lips took hers in a fierce, possessive kiss.

At first Chrissie tried to resist. She squirmed playfully as Drew held her tighter. She struggled to avert her face, to break the contact of their lips, but Drew only ground his harder against hers, until he'd forced her lips to part.

By degrees the rough playfulness ceased. Chrissie stopped struggling. She lifted a hand to caress his cheek, and her body relaxed, softening, burrowing against his with tender capitulation. The kiss gentled, deepening with sensuality. Currents of intense desire flowed through Drew, bringing a terrible, urgent aching in his loins.

His fingers molded over the lush curving thrust of her hip, sliding along her thigh, returning to her bare abdomen and finally rising to stroke one perfectly shaped breast. Chrissie gasped softly, but she did not pull away. Emboldened, Drew's fingers moved to the tender fleshy mound above the fabric of the bikini top and then finally beneath it. He shoved away the strap and the cloth, and ever so lightly his fingers traced a circle around her breast. He felt Chrissie shudder.

Drew broke the kiss, and when he opened his eyes and looked at her, he saw that Chrissie's eyes were glazed. He shifted their positions so that she now lay nestled against the cushion while he leaned over her. With studious deliberation, he untied her bikini top and tossed it aside.

His gaze went to her exposed breasts. They were full, delicately white and ravishingly beautiful. Drew sighed softly, bent his head and kissed the pink bud. Chrissie moaned, and her fingers tightened in his hair.

After a time, Drew bent still lower, and his lips caressed the bare flesh of her midsection. Gently his hands stroked her hips and thighs. Chrissie quivered, and Drew lifted his head. His passion-dark eyes swept her face. "I want you," he said thickly. "Every part of me aches to know every part of you. Make love with me, Chrissie."

Chrissie's eyes smoldered with an answering passion. She inclined her head. Her red-gold crown of hair was like radiant strands of light spun by the last fiery glow of the setting sun. "Yes," she whispered shakily. "Oh, yes, Drew. I've never wanted anything so much as I want you right now."

Drew smiled triumphantly, swooped to kiss her lips once more with wordless promise of joys still to come. When he finally pulled back so that he could look into her eyes again, he saw sensual, open desire for him, and it filled him with an intense happiness he'd never known before. Without prior thought, not knowing he would do it, he smiled with infinite tenderness and unlocked the words that had been imprisoned in his heart. "I love you, Chrissie Barrows. I love you with all of my being."

"Do you?" she asked wistfully. "How do you know for sure?"

"That's easy." His smile deepened. "Because I want to marry you, and the sooner, the better."

Chrissie was so astonished that she sat upright, pushing herself out of his embrace. She stared at him incredulously. "Surely you aren't serious?"

Drew was taken aback at such an unexpected reaction. "Does it really surprise you as much as that? You've been aware of my growing feelings for you from the start, feelings you've certainly given me every reason to believe were fully reciprocated. So what's the matter?"

"The matter," she said in agitation, "is that we hardly even know each other...certainly not well enough to jump into a marriage!"

"But well enough to jump into bed together?"

"That's a nasty thing to say!" Chrissie gasped. She flushed and grabbed for the discarded bikini top but her fumbling fingers couldn't manage the strings. In despair, she tossed it down once more, grabbed the damp towel Drew had dropped next to the chair and draped it around her neck and over her bare breasts.

Swiftly Drew got to his feet. His expression was dark and terrible. "Maybe it was a nasty thing to say, but it's true. You were more than ready to go to bed with me, but the moment I mentioned marriage, you behaved as if I were proposing something indecent!"

Chrissie's throat ached. She was wildly frustrated. "It is! You did! Why did you have to go and spoil things?" she wailed.

"Spoil things?" Drew's eyes narrowed. "How in the hell did I do that? I made an honorable proposal of marriage!"

Chrissie's abrupt anger burned deep. She got to her feet, as well, and lashed out with pure fury. "I'll tell you what I'm getting at! We scarcely know each other, except for the fact that we're obviously physically attracted to each other. We haven't had time to establish any sort of real, ongoing relationship, so how on earth can we possibly know whether we're ready for something so permanent as marriage?" She drew in a shuddering breath, then went straight to the point. "You don't love me! You can't possibly! You're in love with the damned inheritance!"

"Your inheritance?" Drew looked thunderstruck. "Are you crazy?"

"Hardly! The other day you were angry when I told you I wanted to give the money to charity. Now, out of the blue, you up and propose marriage . . . the sooner, the better, you said! I'm sane enough to realize you wouldn't be in quite such a hurry to marry me if I were still just a schoolteacher without a spare dime to my name! You wanted to marry me before I could get rid of the money so you could get your sticky hands on it!"

"Do you hear yourself? Do you honestly believe what you're saying?" Drew was staring at her as though she had grown two heads or something equally bizarre.

"What else can I believe?" she cried stormily. "All this came up mighty fast . . . too fast for me!"

For a long time Drew stood as though frozen, staring at her in silence. His face had gone sickly pale. At last he spoke again, and this time his voice was almost a whisper and Chrissie had to strain to catch his words. "If you can't accept the fact that I'm in love with you . . . that that's the only reason I wanted to marry you, it's evident you don't feel the same for me. If you did, you could never have believed such a thing."

Something in his eyes, an expression of bleak torture, pulled at her heartstrings, but Chrissie was too afraid to trust him so she ignored the powerful instinct she felt to run into his arms. Instead she caught her trembling lower lip between her teeth and looked away.

She heard him sigh softly. "Believe this, then," he said in the same dangerously calm, quiet voice. "You've heard the last of this subject from me. From this moment on, you're just a client, nothing more."

Drew started walking away. Chrissie remained still until she heard the door as he went inside the house. The tears that were choking her throat came out in a shuddering sob.

All at once her confusion and doubts were gone. Drew hadn't lied. She didn't understand how she knew, but the shining truth lay before her. Drew honestly loved her. She'd seen it in his face when she'd assaulted him with her brutal suspicions. He'd been devastated. Even a consummate actor couldn't fake such shock and despair.

Drew loved her. What was more, she loved him. Her previous doubts about her own feelings suddenly evaporated. She was deeply and totally in love with him. Otherwise she could never have been so eager to make love with him. And where was it written, she suddenly asked herself, that two people should know each other a long time before they could be sure that marriage was right for them?

But now the ugly things she'd said to him lay between them. Her suspicions were a lingering result of her previous engagement to a man who'd loved money above all things and later, her paranoia that her inheritance would make her a prey of fortune hunters. The wariness had blinded her to real love so that she hadn't trusted in it when it came her way.

What a fool she'd been! A trembling hand went to her lips, even as she turned around and raced toward the door. Maybe it wasn't too late, yet . . . maybe she could stop Drew and make things right between them. She had to try!

Drew hadn't bothered to change back into his street clothes. When Chrissie entered the back hall, she saw his silhouette emerge from the bathroom with his clothes draped over his arm as he went toward the front door.

"Drew!" she cried. "Wait!" Chrissie began to run.

But Drew kept walking. He opened the front door and went out, shutting the door firmly between them.

Chrissie stopped behind the door, gasping over a sob. There had been something final about the way Drew had closed the door. There was no point in her going after him.

Chapter Eight

The gigantic Sunday edition of the *Los Angeles Times* littered the cocktail table, the floor and the spaces on the sofa surrounding Drew. He groped on the table for his coffee mug, found the handle and brought the rim to his lips while his eyes remained focused on the folded sports section that was balanced across his robe-covered thighs.

When he finished reading the article about a young pro-football hopeful, Drew swallowed the remainder of his coffee and glanced at the wall clock. Seven-forty. It was time to get going, ready or not. Drew shoved aside the newspaper and stood up.

In the bathroom he shed his robe and stepped beneath the shower. In a little less than three hours, he and Chrissie would be meeting Vicky and Paul Nash's flight. The couple had arrived in New York yesterday from London and had spent the night there. It was easier for them to become acclimatized to so many time zone changes that way.

Drew had neither seen nor spoken to Chrissie during the past ten days. The necessary communications between them had been conducted through his secretary. If it wasn't part of his job to meet with Vicky, he wouldn't go near Chrissie today, but business was business. He would get through it somehow.

The arrangement was for him to pick up Chrissie and they would go together to meet the Nashes' plane. Over a private luncheon at the mansion, Drew would give Vicky an overall view of her inheritance before she met later in the week with the others at the office, just as he had done with Chrissie when he'd visited her in New Orleans. Afterward he would remain to help entertain the couple, especially Paul. Around five o'clock, the invited guests would begin arriving for a poolside buffet party in the British couple's honor.

Actually, seeing Chrissie today probably wouldn't be that much of an ordeal. Ever since the moment she'd accused him of wanting to marry her for the money, Drew's emotions had become hardened by a thick layer of ice. He felt nothing toward her whatsoever, not love, not anger, not pain. Just...nothing.

The irony of her unjust charge did not escape Drew. Carol had jilted *him* because he didn't have enough money to suit her notions of grandeur; then, along comes Chrissie, indicting him of plotting to marry *her* for her money! It was hilariously funny, a huge joke, but Drew was too numb to laugh.

Maybe someday he would find the right woman, one who wasn't obsessed about money. At the moment, though, he wasn't convinced he ever wanted to get involved with another woman, much less marry one, no matter what her attitude was about money. Drew earned a more-than-respectable salary already, and his future earning potential was even more promising. If he ever did marry, most certainly he could support a wife in comfort. He might not be able to give her uncounted millions as Carol had wanted, but he could easily provide a very good living for a family without needing his wife to contribute one cent. His wife would be able to work outside the home or not, as she chose. He had neither the desire nor the need to marry any woman for her financial worth. Such a thought had never entered his mind until Chrissie had so astonishingly accused him of it.

Drew turned off the shower, stepped onto the bath mat and reached for a towel. When he was dry, he turned to the washbasin and began to shave.

He eyed himself indifferently in the mirror as he ran the razor over his jaw. He forced his thoughts away from Chrissie. There was still one bright spot in his life—the Wellington case. More than ever Drew was grateful he'd been given the assignment. This was the sort of case he'd always dreamed of, and now with women out of his life completely—for the time being, anyway—he could concentrate on his job fully, without any distractions.

Fifteen minutes later, dressed in slacks, a white knit polo shirt topped by a casual tan jacket, he left the apartment. Throughout the drive to Bel Air, with the same self-control he'd exerted earlier, Drew kept his thoughts on anything other than the woman he was about to see.

When he reached the mansion, parked and walked to the door, his feelings remained buried beneath a thick, crusted layer of ice. Drew pressed the doorbell and waited.

Chrissie opened the door. Drew was presented with a vision of feminine loveliness at its finest. She wore a white summer dress with bits of dainty lace here and there and a pink braided belt around her tiny waist. Her throat and shoulders were bare, and her hair was a cloud of red-tinged gold surrounding her face. Her eyes today were a deep Pacific blue, and her soft, delicate lips were rosebud pink.

Briefly, ever so briefly, some of the ice melted within Drew's heart, and he was as drawn to her as ever. But almost immediately his self-defense mechanism swung back into action, saving him, and he could actually look at her dispassionately.

"Morning," he said with a crisp nod of his head.

"Good morning." Chrissie's voice was soft and low, slightly breathless, and her eyes were voluminous as she gazed at him. "Won't... won't you come in?"

"We don't have much time to spare before the flight is due, especially if we run into heavy traffic. If you're ready, we'd better go."

"All right. I'll just get my purse."

Chrissie left the door open as she turned and crossed the foyer to the long table where she'd placed her bag. When she picked it up, she paused for an instant, squeezed her eyes shut and inhaled deeply. There was something different about Drew today. There was a hard shell around him that dashed her hopes. She sighed and, girding herself for the difficult ordeal ahead, turned and walked toward him.

Today should be the happiest day of her life—the day she would finally meet her twin sister face-to-face. She *was* happy about that! It was only that the happiness was tempered by the estrangement that existed between herself and Drew. She had harbored an optimism that today she might manage to bridge the distance, but with one look at his face, the hopes were beginning to crumble.

But some hopes die hard, and Chrissie wasn't ready to give up in defeat without at least making a strong effort. She had only herself to blame for this situation, and it was up to her to change it if she could. Perhaps a drive to the airport wasn't ideal for a heart-to-heart talk with Drew, but it was the only time she was likely to be granted in the foreseeable future. They would be alone together only until they reached the airport. After that she might never have the opportunity again.

Since that disastrous scene following Drew's proposal, Chrissie had had more than enough time to repent her rash words. Drew's profound shock couldn't possibly have been faked, even if he'd been an accomplished actor. His face had gone a deathly white, and the raw pain glazing his eyes had been genuine. She had falsely accused him of ugly, calculated intentions based on nothing more than the timing of his proposal. Her insidious suspicions had marred the fine, beautiful clarity of real love. She had done a terrible thing, and now she had to try to repair the damage if she could.

Drew was not going to make it easy for her. As he started the car and drove through the gate, the tension between them was as thick as a heavy fog rolling in from the ocean. He looked straight ahead as he drove, and the profile of his face was rigidly outlined against the sunlit window. He made no effort to speak to her.

Despite the strong negative vibrations, Chrissie didn't allow herself to be put off. It was now or never.

"Drew?" The word came out thin and insubstantial. Chrissie inhaled and tried a second time. "Drew?"

"What is it?" Drew did not turn his head toward her, and his voice was cold and brusque.

It was definitely not an inviting opening, but it was the only one she'd been given. Nervously Chrissie plunged ahead. "About the other day—the last time we were together. I want to apologize...."

She broke off, unsure how to continue, hoping, too, to get some response from him. There was none. It was as though she hadn't even spoken.

After an uncomfortable silence, Chrissie forced herself to go on. "I was wrong...so very wrong. I know that now. I beg your forgiveness, Drew. Please."

"Sure," he responded indifferently. "No problem."

His acceptance of her apology came too glibly, too easily. "Do you really mean it?" she asked huskily.

Drew shrugged carelessly. "Why not? It was no big deal."

"You proposed marriage and it was no big deal?" Chrissie's voice was anguished.

Drew merely shrugged again.

"Why not?" Chrissie pressed for an explanation.

"Because you brought me to my senses and made me see what a dumb mistake I'd made."

Pain lodged in Chrissie's chest and throat. "You...you said you loved me. Was that true?"

"I just told you...the whole thing was a mistake." Drew's voice was sharp and impatient. "Look, I'm not much on rehashing the past. Why don't we forget it?"

"Because...I'm trying to tell you that I love you."

This time Drew did look at her, but there was no softening of his expression. His eyes flashed with scorn, and his tone was hard. "I doubt that. I doubt very much whether you even know the meaning of the word."

"I do!" she cried. "What does it take for you to believe me?"

Drew shook his head. "Sweetheart," he said sarcastically, "maybe you think that's what you feel, but I don't want your particular brand of love. If a woman can't trust in me completely, I certainly have no place for her in my life. I've got my pride...integrity, too, in spite of your low opinion of me...and I intend to hang on to both."

"You'd rather let pride get in the way of love?" Chrissie asked bitterly.

"What love?" he demanded. His voice was angry now. "The person I thought I fell in love with didn't actually exist. If she had, you'd never have doubted me in the first place. And I just told you...you can't really be in love with me or you wouldn't have thought those things. So whatever we did feel for each other was sex, pure and simple."

He tossed her a hateful glance and added, "While I might still be enticed into your bed, given the invitation, I can guarantee you I won't be gullible enough to invite you a second time to be my wife!"

Chrissie sucked in an unsteady breath. Drew's cruel words were like a physical assault. She'd tried to prepare herself for his rejection, but she hadn't expected him to be this cutting. She was devastated, and it was all she could do to hold back the tears that were bottled inside her throat.

She turned her head toward the side window so that Drew couldn't see if the tears did come. Oh, God, what a fool she was! She couldn't have picked a worse time to try to talk to him! He was as hard as nails, and now she couldn't get away from him when all she longed to do was to go off by herself and lick her wounds.

She should never have admitted she was in love with him after he was so flippant about her apology. She should have realized he would only attack her with her own words. Idiotically she had dared to hope he cared enough to accept her apology, to take her declaration of love at face value and put an end to the loneliness and pain they'd both endured.

As it turned out, only she had been lonely and suffering. Drew had nursed hostility and resentment. If he ever had loved her, it had now crystallized into a stone of absolute contempt.

No more words passed between them before they reached the airport, and for that, Chrissie was grateful. She needed every moment to mentally and emotionally pull herself together before greeting her sister. She couldn't have managed if the disturbing conversation had resumed, nor if Drew had merely attempted to make small talk. At least he was kind enough to spare her that!

When they arrived at the proper gate, it was with ten minutes to spare. Drew broke the strained silence between them and said prosaically, "There are a couple of empty seats. We may as well sit down."

Chrissie nodded and preceded him to the empty lounge chairs. She carefully refrained from looking at him as they sat down, and then she clasped her hands in her lap and fixed her gaze on the door through which the incoming passengers would be walking.

Five minutes went by before Drew broke the silence again. "Chrissie?"

"Yes?" She tensed.

"I think it'll be best all around if we try to bury our differences when we're with your sister and her husband. No good can come from making them feel uncomfortable."

Stiffly Chrissie nodded. "I agree."

"Good. Let's keep it light and loose, then."

"Right." She nodded again. "Light and loose." Chrissie didn't have a clue how to accomplish that, given the battered and bruised condition of her mind just now, but it sounded great in theory.

When the plane finally taxied up to the terminal building and an airline employee opened the door to the ramp, Chrissie's heart thudded. She rose to her feet. The imminent reunion with her twin abruptly superceded the turmoil of her relationship with Drew. She was suddenly happy, excited and strangely terrified.

Drew rose, too, and clasped her trembling hand. Dazed, Chrissie turned toward him. For the first time today, he had a smile for her. "You're shaking," he observed. "And your hand is cold."

"I'm . . . afraid."

"Of what?"

"Everything. What if we don't recognize each other? What if she hates me?"

Drew chuckled softly. "She's your identical twin. How can you not recognize her? And you've talked on the phone several times and gotten along just fine, haven't you? Why would she hate you?"

"I don't know. But what if..."

Drew squeezed her icy fingers with his warmer ones. In spite of everything that had gone between them, his touch was comforting and somehow it eased her nerves. "Shh," he whispered soothingly. "Everything will be great, you'll see."

The first of the deplaning passengers trickled through the doorway. Despite Drew's encouragement, Chrissie's whole body was tense.

A young couple came into view. Chrissie scarcely noted the man, save that he sported a short brown beard and had a camera dangling from a strap around his neck. Her entire attention was centered on the woman at his side. She was dressed conservatively in a beige skirt and jacket and a sea-green blouse. Shoulder-length red-gold hair waved riotously about her face—a face that was a replica of Chrissie's own.

Chrissie gasped softly. Drew released her hand, and winged feet carried her across the lounge. Seeing her, Vicky cried out, dropped her carry-on bag and spread her arms as she rushed to meet Chrissie.

The twins met in a crushing embrace. Sometime later, trembling, they drew apart in order to gaze into each other's faces. Laughing and crying at the same time, they fervently embraced again.

Drew watched the emotionally charged scene with a sympathetic smile. In spite of the end of things between himself and Chrissie, he couldn't help but be overjoyed for her at this moment. Only someone without a heart could have remained untouched.

But at last his attention shifted to a man about his own age who stood to one side of the two women. Only the man's brown hair and part of his beard were visible; the rest of his face was hidden behind a camera as he snapped photographs of the dramatic reunion.

Drew went to join him. "You must be Paul Nash."

The camera lowered, and the other man turned toward him with a smile. "That's right."

"My name's Casey. Drew Casey. I'm the attorney who was in charge of tracking down your wife."

The two men shook hands. "It's a pleasure to meet you," Paul Nash said.

"Same here." Drew's gaze shifted from Paul back to the twins. They had ceased hugging at last and were now engaged in animated conversation. Both of them appeared to be talking as fast as they could, as though they had to hurry before the other sister vanished.

Drew turned to Nash again and grinned. "You suppose we can break that up long enough to get them out of here?"

"All we can do is try," Paul replied with a grin of his own. He stepped forward and interrupted. "We're still here, too, ladies," he informed them. "And I'm getting impatient to meet my sister-in-law."

Vicky and Chrissie both laughed and turned their teary-eyed faces toward the men. Chrissie and Paul embraced briefly after their introduction; Vicky and Drew cordially shook hands.

With determined effort, the men finally got their little group to baggage claim, and at long last into the car. Chrissie and Vicky chose to sit together in the back seat. Paul good-naturedly accepted his temporary banishment from his wife's side and climbed into the front next to Drew.

"I can't believe this is really happening," said Vicky, smiling at Chrissie. "It's like a dream. A beautiful, lovely dream."

"I know," Chrissie answered huskily. "Only better, because it's real!"

Paul twisted in his seat to look back at them with an amused smile. "It was hard for me to credit at first—Vicky's having an identical twin—but you're most definitely two peas from the same pod. I'm beginning to worry how I'm going to tell you apart."

Vicky giggled. "It would be fun if we could fool him sometime, wouldn't it?"

Chrissie laughed and nodded. "I've got a suspicion you have nothing to worry about, Paul. Not many people are ever going to mistake my American accent for Vicky's British one—and more's the pity."

"We'll practice each other's accents," Vicky declared.

Paul rolled his eyes and turned to Drew. "I can tell already they're exactly alike when it comes to mischief."

"You'd better be on guard," Drew said with a grin. "You could be in for double trouble! Maybe they can't fool you with their voices, but they might find other ways."

"Don't put ideas into their heads!" Paul exclaimed.

The drive back to the mansion was accomplished with much lighthearted banter. Chrissie and Vicky were wholeheartedly enjoying each other. There was plenty of time ahead to get acquainted, and serious discussions would come later. Today was for the pure pleasure of being together.

The only serious conversation at all came over lunch, during which Drew described the extent of Laura Douglas's estate for Vicky and Paul's benefit. Specific details would be addressed later in the week when the couple visited the law firm.

When Drew finished speaking, Vicky appeared stunned. Paul also looked as though he were in a state of shock. "Did...did I understand you to say...m-millions?" Vicky stammered. "More than one?"

Drew nodded. "We don't yet have an exact accounting down to the last cent, but even rounded off and divided in half with Chrissie, it's safe to say your share will be a tidy little sum."

"That's a slight understatement, wouldn't you say, old chap?" Paul murmured. His wife looked at him helplessly, and he extended his hand to her. "We understood from Mr. Chamberlain in London that there was a good bit of money involved, but we thought perhaps a couple of hundred thousand pounds at most . . . certainly nothing of this magnitude."

Vicky's gaze went to Chrissie, and her voice was accusing. "You could've warned me when we talked on the telephone."

"I was overwhelmed when I first learned about it myself," Chrissie explained. "I thought it was better to wait and let you hear it from Drew rather than me."

"But . . . so much, and from a woman I never knew? Somehow it doesn't seem right."

Drew sighed. "You, too? Your sister feels that way. I was hoping you'd be a little happier about it. After all, Miss Douglas was your mother. Who has a better right to inherit her fortune than her own children?"

"I understand the logic of it," Vicky replied. "It's just that I'm having a difficult time accepting the fact that she *was* my mother. She was famous, even in England, and yet my father never breathed a word about her to me."

"You said your father was possessive about you," Paul reminded her. "Plainly he never wanted you to know. He didn't want to have to share you with her."

Vicky sighed. "I suppose. This is all a great shock, you know. It's going to take some getting used to. I'm not sure I'll ever believe it!"

Paul leaned toward her and asked softly, "Do you have a difficult time accepting that Chrissie is your twin sister?"

"Of course not!" she exclaimed. "I only have to look at her to see myself. That's true, all right!"

Paul grinned. "Then the rest of it must be, too. Your father never told you anything before he died, so who else except your own mother could have known you were twins and brought you together like this? And as Drew pointed out, who else was she to leave her fortune to, except for the two of you?"

Vicky frowned at her husband. "I hate it when you make sense!" Everyone laughed, but then in a serious vein she asked Chrissie, "Has all this been shocking and difficult for you to come to terms with, too?"

"I could write you a book," Chrissie muttered. "Just wait until your meeting with the other attorneys and the accountants. It gets worse. As for coming to terms with it . . . I haven't." She kept her eyes carefully averted from Drew. Between them the subject of money was thorny, to say the least.

"I can't imagine what we'll do with so much money," Vicky murmured. "Except that we'll be able to afford a place in the country that we've only dreamed about until now."

Paul grinned. "I have this strong feeling you'll manage to spend a sizable chunk of it on frequent plane trips to America now that you've discovered Chrissie."

"Not to mention paying the telephone bills." Chrissie's grin was even broader.

"Ouch! That's the truth!" Paul winced as though he were in pain and told Drew, "Vicky's first call to Chrissie lasted nearly three hours! I was watching the clock and having a heart attack at the same time, but did my extravagant wife have even a shred of sympathy?"

Drew laughed. "I can see you'll need all the money then to keep her in transatlantic phone calls and airline tickets. I suppose that's just how it is with long-lost twins. They've got a lot of years to catch up on."

"Yeah." Paul's gaze was tender as he looked at his wife's glowing face. Then he smiled at Chrissie. "That's just how it is...every Christmas, birthday and holiday rolled into one. I wouldn't trade Vicky's happiness over discovering Chrissie for a hundred fortunes, even if I had to work a second job to pay off that telephone bill. It's good to have you in the family, Chrissie."

"Thanks," Chrissie replied huskily. Vicky was fortunate to have a husband like Paul Nash—a warmhearted, understanding man. Anyone could see that he adored his wife and that she felt the same way about him. Chrissie was glad for Vicky, although her sister's marriage poignantly illustrated what she herself might have had with Drew if it hadn't been for her stupid, unfounded suspicions.

When the meal was over, Drew and Paul opted to stroll the grounds, leaving the twins alone together for a couple of hours. The sisters went upstairs, and while Vicky unpacked in the Mexican bedroom, Chrissie kept her company.

Much of the time they talked of their separate childhoods, each trying to fill in the blanks of their lives for the other. Then Chrissie asked about their father. "What was he like? Was he really possessive of you?"

Vicky nodded. "Very. He didn't like for me to get too chummy with my schoolmates or be away from home very long at a time. I never even went on a date until after I was grown. Father was a quiet, bookish man, and yet he was affectionate, and I always knew he loved me. It was just that sometimes it felt as though his love was smothering me." She sighed and sat down on the bed next to Chrissie. "Now...with all these new revelations, I suppose I can understand why. Mother went away forever and took you with her. I was all he had left."

"What explanation did he give you about your mother...our mother?" Chrissie asked quietly.

Vicky shook her head. "I was always under the impression that she had died in America. Whether Father told me that when I was quite young or merely hinted at it, I don't recall. He wasn't an easy man to talk to on an intimate level, and I never really pressed him for details. Now I see that I should have. I'm ... I'm very angry that he never told me about you!" Her lip trembled. "I'm not sure I'll ever be able to forgive him."

Chrissie nodded. "I've felt that way about Laura, especially since she placed me for adoption instead of returning me to Father and you." She glanced at her watch. "Enough of that for now! If you're going to change into that pretty dress you bought yesterday in New York, you'd better be fast. Our guests will be arriving in another half hour."

Vicky slid off the bed, unbuttoning her blouse. "Who are the people we'll be meeting?"

"I invited everyone at Pitts, Smythe and Raleigh, and of course their wives, husbands or dates. And Drew's family."

"Oh?" Vicky's voice was frankly interested. "Why Drew's family? Do you two have some sort of relationship going? I got the distinct impression that there was something going on. Both of you were awfully busy trying not to look at each other except when it was absolutely necessary."

"You saw that, did you?" Chrissie asked glumly. She was too miserable about the state of affairs between her and Drew to pretend anymore. "There was something between us for a while," she admitted honestly. "But I ruined it."

"He seems like a nice man," Vicky said speculatively. "Charming, actually." She tossed aside her blouse, slid out of her skirt and reached for the pastel print dress she'd draped across the back of a chair.

"He is," Chrissie conceded. "Charming and nice. Very nice. The trouble is that I couldn't see that for myself until it was too late."

"Are you in—" Vicky's question hung suspended in the air because there was a knock on the door.

A moment later Paul Nash's head poked around the door. "Mind if I come in?" he asked. "Some people just pulled into the drive, and Drew went out to welcome them. I wanted to come wash my face and grab my wife before I meet them."

Hastily Chrissie headed for the door. "I'd better go down at once."

A minute later she joined Drew on the wide front veranda just as John Keene and his wife came toward the steps.

The California-style buffet party was a sparkling success. A few guests made use of the pool while others lounged nearby, eating, drinking or chatting. Alice and Betsy served a delicious selection of food, and Drew, without being asked, took charge as cohost and served drinks. Chrissie appreciated his thoughtfulness. It left her free to mingle with her guests and see to it that everyone was comfortable.

All the guests were friendly to Vicky and Paul, and Chrissie was satisfied that they were enjoying themselves. Vicky seemed especially drawn to Drew's mother, Maggie, just as Chrissie was herself. The entire Casey family was as warm and outgoing as they'd been the evening Drew had taken Chrissie to his mother's home. Because she liked them so well, Chrissie was saddened to realize that after today it was unlikely she would ever be with them again.

When the party finally wound to an end and the guests said goodbye, Drew again stood beside Chrissie. On her other side were Paul and Vicky, arms about each other's waists. It was a casual yet provocatively intimate contact. It stated loud and clear that the couple had the right to touch, that they were a team, that they fully trusted each other. Chrissie's throat ached as she yearned to have the right to touch Drew so confidently, to be that secure within his love. Instead she had nothing of him.

When the last guests were gone, Paul and Vicky said good-night. Fatigue was telling in both their faces.

"It was a lovely party," Vicky said.

"We enjoyed meeting everyone," Paul told them as he tried to fight a yawn. "But if you don't mind, we'll be going to bed now. We're exhausted."

"Good night," Drew told them.

"Sleep well," Chrissie said. She and Drew both watched in silence as the other couple went up the stairs.

When they were completely alone, Drew said in a strained voice, "I'll be leaving now, too. Good night."

He half turned, but Chrissie hastily placed a hand on his arm. "I want to thank you for all you did today," she said softly. "For everything."

Drew's marble-hard eyes met hers briefly, and then he shrugged. "There's nothing to thank me for. I was only doing my job."

His cold rejection of her attempts to thank him couldn't have been harsher than a slap in the face. Chrissie inhaled deeply with pain, unconsciously straightened her shoulders and nodded. "Of course." She spoke in a crisp voice. "I realized that. Good night, Drew."

She had hurt Drew down to his soul by flinging her ill-considered accusations at him when he'd been offering her his life and his heart. There was to be no real forgiveness, much less a reconciliation. Somehow she would have to learn to live with it.

Chrissie locked the door after Drew left, turned out the light and, with heavy despair, went upstairs to bed.

Chapter Nine

Per-r-r-fect! Now...smile!'' Paul Nash shouted from behind his camera.

The twins, both wearing shorts, tank tops and with their hair whipping wildly in the wind, sat on the beach next to a somewhat lopsided sand castle they had constructed. Behind them roared the Pacific and above them was a brilliant blue cloudless sky. On cue, following Paul's command, they smiled and he snapped the picture.

For the past week nearly all their time had been spent on short sight-seeing excursions around the Los Angeles area or on more serious photographic forays into the nearby mountains, canyons and points along the ocean highway north of Malibu. Chrissie had discovered that Paul was not only a professional photographer with a keen eye, but that he was also a compulsive shutterbug. Already he'd taken at least a couple of hundred shots of Vicky and Chrissie, formal and informal as they ate by candlelight, pored over business papers with Jane, got in and out of the car at various locations around town, talked on the telephone or took a walk. No circumstance seemed too mundane for Paul to record on film. By the time he returned to England, he would have a complete photographic diary of his stay in California and of the twins' first visit with each other.

Satisfied at last with these latest shots, Paul joined the twins and sat down on a beach towel beside Vicky. "You girls are getting so good at posing, you could easily become professional models if you wanted. It must come naturally. After all, Laura was a model when she first met your father."

"Not interested," Vicky stated flatly. "I'll do it for our family photo album, but that's my limit. All that smiling makes my face hurt!"

"Mine, too," Chrissie seconded. "When you two return to London, I may never smile again. By the way, Vicky, speaking of photo albums, remind me tonight to show you Laura's."

"What album?"

"I found it in her bedroom closet. It's mostly pictures of me while I was growing up, but there are a few baby photos of the two of us."

"How did she get them?" Vicky asked in surprise.

"Apparently she brought the baby pictures with her when she returned to the U.S. following the divorce. As for mine..." Chrissie shrugged. "My adoptive mother sent them to her."

"Hmm. I definitely want to see this album, though it's rather difficult to think of a Laura Douglas maternal enough to preserve a book full of children's photographs, don't you agree?"

"Very difficult," Chrissie said, nodding. "Finding the album did a lot to mellow my feelings about her, even though I still can't really think of her as my mother. I doubt I ever will."

"Neither can I," Vicky responded. Thoughtfully she added, "You actually *have* a real mother in your life, so it's logical you can't think of Laura in such terms. But I don't even know what it's like to have a mother of any sort. When I was growing up, the only women in my life were house-keepers, and there were several of them through the years. There was never any one woman there for me for any length of time."

Chrissie smiled gently. "I promise I'll share mine with you when she gets here. She'll be delighted to have another daughter to fuss over. Dad, too."

Chrissie had persuaded Jack and Marie to fly out and spend a long weekend so that they could meet Vicky and Paul before they returned to England next week. They would be arriving in just a few more days.

"I'm looking forward to meeting your parents," Paul told Chrissie.

"Of course." She chuckled. "They'll be a couple of new faces to photograph."

Paul grinned, silently acknowledging the truth of the statement.

"I'm eager to meet them, too," Vicky said. "From everything you've told us about them, they sound like won-derful people."

"They are," Chrissie agreed. "The absolute best."

"What time is it getting to be?" Vicky asked, suddenly changing the subject. She turned to her husband. "If you don't take me someplace to eat soon, I'll be malnourished and weak by the time Chrissie's parents arrive, and then they'll think you're an abusive husband. All this posing is hard work, and I'm starving!"

"Me, too!" Chrissie chimed in.

Paul sighed and shook his head. "All I ever seem to do is feed you two! I think we've checked out every restaurant in southern California! Get fat and I won't take your pictures anymore.''

"Is that a promise?" Chrissie teased.

They stopped for hamburgers on the drive back to the city, and it was midafternoon when they got to the mansion. Jane White greeted them with the news that John Keene had telephoned to arrange a meeting with both twins. "The accountants and the management firm have finally worked out their in-depth reports, and they're ready to put forward their suggestions concerning the best way to settle the estate. Mr. Keene and the other attorneys will be able to fill you in about probate. He suggested two o'clock tomorrow afternoon, if that's agreeable with you."

"It's fine with me," Vicky said. "Chrissie?"

Chrissie nodded and told Jane, "Call John Keene back and tell him we'll be there."

She went upstairs to shower off the beach sand and wondered whether Drew would be present at the meeting. She had neither seen him nor heard from him since the night of the buffet party over a week ago. Last week Vicky and Paul had seen him when they'd visited the law office for their initial meeting with the entire group of lawyers, but Chrissie's presence hadn't been required that day.

At least having Vicky and Paul around this past week had helped keep her brooding about Drew to a minimum. That was all to the good, because the times when she was utterly alone were sheer hell.

She kept her pain concealed behind a cheerful attitude during the day while she was with her sister. She was determined not to inflict Vicky and Paul with the burden of her unhappiness. It wouldn't be fair to them. But at night in the dark privacy of her bedroom when no one could witness the tears, Chrissie allowed her true feelings to surface. It was during those hours that she realized the depths of her love for Drew, a love so powerful that it astonished her. Until now, she'd never known love could be this strong, so high, so wide, so deep, so unshakable. It was an entity entirely of itself, separate from her and yet a part of her, and she had become conscious of the absolute certainty that her love for Drew would be her constant companion for the rest of her life.

Her thoughts were so depressing that Chrissie rushed through her shower. The less time she spent alone, the better. As soon as she had dressed in a cotton skirt and blouse, she returned downstairs.

At the conclusion of dinner later that evening, Vicky reminded Chrissie about Laura's photo album. "Can we look at it now?"

"Sure. Do you want to come upstairs to Laura's room with me, or should I bring it down?"

"Why don't you go upstairs with her?" Paul suggested to Vicky. "I want to watch television."

"What? You don't want to see the entire photo history of my childhood?" Chrissie teased. "And you, a photographer? I'm hurt, Paul. Really hurt."

Paul grinned unrepentently. "Some other time. I want to see this detective program. American telly detectives are always so brilliant and tough. I wonder how it is that they come through without a scratch week after week after week?"

"Amazing, isn't it?" Chrissie laughed.

The twins went up to Laura's bedroom while Paul headed for the den. Chrissie got the album from the closet, and she and Vicky settled back against the mound of pillows at the head of Laura's king-sized bed.

It was a pleasant half hour. Vicky chuckled over some of the photos of a young Chrissie and demanded explanations for each memento. Chrissie complied, elaborating on a skating contest here, a birthday party there and even on a couple of family vacations.

When they were nearing the last pages, Vicky shook her head in wonder. "I can't get over this! It's like looking back over my own childhood pictures, right down to the ever-present scrapes and scratches. Say, I like your dog," she said, peering closer at a shot of Chrissie around the age of eight with a shaggy brown-haired dog. "He looks a lot like one I had. What did you call him?"

"Mops."

Vicky squealed with delight. "So was mine!" She sobered abruptly. "God, Chrissie, it's downright spooky how much we've always been alike!"

"I know." Chrissie groaned with fresh agony over the irreplaceable loss of their years spent apart. "I feel so cheated that we weren't allowed to grow up together."

"So do I," Vicky murmured softly.

"What I can't understand is why Laura didn't send me back to England," Chrissie said. "Why she put me up for adoption instead."

"If she was broke, as well as ill, like your parents said, I can see she couldn't afford such an expensive trip," Vicky mused. "But if that was the case, why didn't she simply ask Father for the money? I'm sure he would have sent it to her!"

Restlessly Chrissie slipped off the bed and walked to the window. "I can't imagine. It's the one thing that I find so unforgivable."

Behind her, Vicky sighed, and then Chrissie heard the raspy sound of another page turning.

"Hey...what's this?"

"What?" Chrissie left the window and went back to stand next to the bed.

"It's an envelope taped to the inside back cover!" Vicky tore the tape away, stared at the envelope for a moment and then offered it to Chrissie. "It's addressed to you. Laura must have written you a letter!"

Chrissie's mouth went dry. Weakly she sank to the edge of the bed and opened the brittle age-yellowed envelope with trembling fingers. She scanned the contents, and a moment later she cried out and handed the letter to Vicky. "Read it!" she gasped. "Oh, Vicky, she *did* try to get me back to you and Father! She tried!"

Vicky hastily read the letter herself. Finally she said quietly. "Well... now we know."

Chrissie nodded, unable to speak.

Laura had written a brief explanation about why the twins had been separated. Since Laura would be living in the United States, she and Nigel felt it was only fair that each parent have custody of one child. Because the girls would be growing up so far apart, they had been trying to spare the girls hard feelings and divided loyalties by agreeing never to tell them they each had a twin sister. It was only much later when Laura finally came to believe the agreement had been wrong.

As to Chrissie's adoption, Laura had chosen that course only as a last, desperate resort. Ill and without funds, she had first tried to contact her ex-husband, but Nigel had moved and left no forwarding address. Even his publishers had no current address for him at that time. So Laura had placed Chrissie with Jack and Marie Barrows with the understanding that she would always be kept informed about her daughter. Given her circumstances, it was the best she could do, both for herself and for Chrissie.

"We moved several times when I was young," Vicky confirmed now. "When Father was researching a specific locale for one of his books, we would move there for a year or two. Knowing what a private man he was, I can see that it's entirely possible that there were indeed times when even his publishers didn't know where he was. It was only after I was of school age that we settled for good in a small village within easy traveling distance to London."

"And by then," Chrissie said huskily, taking back the letter, "when Father had published more books and Laura could have contacted him, it was too late. Legally I belonged to another family, and she couldn't see any good in telling anyone the truth...not our father or you or me. It would only have brought anguish to everyone."

Vicky nodded. "So she chose this way to let us know about each other's existence...after both Father and she were gone. Maybe it was the wisest course, Chrissie."

"Maybe it was at that." Chrissie read aloud the final sentence of the letter Laura had written. "'I never stopped loving my daughters every day of my life, even though it had to be from a distance. I can only hope you both will forgive me and your father for what we did. It was never our intention for anyone to be hurt.'"

"I can forgive them everything, because in the end she brought us together," Vicky said softly. "But can you?"

Chrissie's eyes shimmered. "Yes," she whispered. "They did what they thought was fair for everyone when they separated. Now that I know Laura did want to return me to Father and you before she gave me up for good, the last of my bitterness is gone. My adoptive parents are truly loving parents, and I can never be sorry that I was raised as their daughter. I adore them. It was just believing that Laura hadn't wanted me or cared enough about me to send me back to my own family that was so painful. Knowing the truth has finally freed me completely of the past."

Vicky smiled and abruptly slid off the bed. "Let's go show this letter to Paul. We've just solved the mystery of our lives, and it's far more interesting than his dumb old detective show!"

The following afternoon Chrissie, Vicky and Paul entered the spacious paneled conference room at Pitts, Smythe and Raleigh. A long, highly polished table dominated the center of the room, but no one was yet seated at it. A number of people were already present, standing around talking in small groups.

Chrissie had thought she was braced for the likelihood of seeing Drew, but she found that she wasn't. The instant she entered the room, despite the other people there, she was conscious only of him.

Drew stood at one end of the room with a man she recognized as being from the management firm, and Drew's back was toward her. Her eyes automatically traced the outline of his head, noting the neat lay of his dark hair. He was once again wearing the gray business suit she admired, and her gaze took in the breadth of his well-shaped shoulders and the tapering of his long legs before, catching her breath, she forced herself to look away. It would never do to let Drew find her staring at him.

John Keene came forward to greet the newcomers, followed by Bob Raleigh. With the greatest concentration, Chrissie summoned a passable smile and focused her attention on them.

One by one the other men in the room came to speak to them. Inevitably it was Drew's turn.

He first greeted Paul and Vicky, and then he turned toward Chrissie and extended his hand for a formal handshake. Unwillingly Chrissie gave her hand to him. When he clasped it, Drew's grip was firm, but his fingers were cold and he touched her only briefly before releasing her hand.

"Glad you could make it today."

The meaningless, polite words seemed to fall easily from Drew's lips, yet Chrissie scarcely heard them. Her attention was on his eyes, where a now-familiar blank wall had been thrown up. He was looking directly at her, and yet Chrissie could have sworn that he didn't see her at all—because he chose not to see her. No light illuminated the forest-brown depths of his eyes. There was only a dull, flat, opaque lack of any emotion whatsoever.

Chrissie yearned to bring back his old, easygoing, natural smile, to restore to his eyes the light that had once been there. She ached to touch his hand and find it warm and responsive. Toward her, at least, it was as though the very essence of life had gone out of Drew. It was her fault, and she wanted to change it, yet she didn't know what she could do.

The desperation of her own love for him swelled inside her, tightening her throat, beating painfully in her heart, surging through her veins. If only Drew would forgive her, could believe that she loved him, that she was truly sorry for her accusations, she would gladly spend the rest of her life making it up to him. The only thing she wanted was the chance. But when she'd tried, Drew had refused to listen. There was nothing more she could do.

Yet some stubborn part of her resisted meekly accepting that their budding love was really gone forever. There had to be a way to penetrate the icy shield around Drew's emotions; there had to be a way to make him listen, to show him how much she cared. There had to be a way to make him see what a terrible mistake he was making for both of them by shutting her out.

But for the present, she was helpless. Already Drew had withdrawn from her and was speaking again with Paul.

John Keene was suddenly at her side, touching her elbow. "Why don't you sit down, Chrissie? The accountants are waiting until you and Vicky are seated."

"Of course." Fully jolted back to what was required of her at the moment, Chrissie stepped forward and allowed John to pull out a chair for her. Vicky came to sit beside her an instant later, and then there was a general movement as all the men took their places.

Bob Raleigh took his seat at the head of the table and opened the meeting. For the next forty-five minutes there were oral reports from accountants and the representatives from the realty management firm concerning the current status of taxes, profits and losses from the varied interests that made up the estate. John Keene gave a rundown on stock and bond holdings. Following each brief report came questions from the attorneys or from Vicky, Paul or Chrissie. The Nashes asked the most questions because of their difficulty in understanding American tax laws.

When the reports were finally over, the meeting continued on to the next item on the agenda—the breakdown and ultimate disposition of individual holdings. Each of the experts had advice and suggestions to make. Some investments were considered a drain and the twins were advised to liquidate them; others it was felt should be maintained. The question was whether the twins wished to form a partnership and own all properties jointly, or have a legal division of the entire estate.

For the first time, Drew spoke up. "It's been my understanding that Miss Barrows prefers to liquidate her share so that she'll have no further responsibility to the estate. In light of this, it seems reasonable that Mrs. Nash should be given first refusal on the purchase of her sister's interest in any property she might prefer to retain."

"Certainly that would be the most proper and equitable way to handle it," John Keene said. "This rather takes me by surprise, however." He looked directly at Chrissie. "Miss Barrows, I had no idea you wanted to dispose of everything."

Equally surprised, Vicky turned to Chrissie and asked with astonishment, "Is this true? Do you really want to sell out your interest in everything?"

Chrissie wished Drew hadn't brought up the subject, but she couldn't whip up any anger toward him. He had only been expressing what she had so vehemently insisted to him that she wanted. But his objections had belatedly had the effect of causing her to seriously rethink her position. Accordingly she'd begun a self-prescribed course of late-night studying, and she was slowly beginning to understand the principles of the stock market, real estate and general business management practices. She fully realized that it would be an uphill battle to become proficient in the world of finance and investment, but she had made up her mind that not only would she learn, she would put what she learned to practical use.

Now she laced her fingers together on the table in front of her. "It *was* true at one time, but not any longer." Chrissie met Vicky's eyes as she continued earnestly. "I've been doing a lot of studying, and while I know I still have worlds yet to learn and that I'm going to need a lot of help and guidance along the way, I've decided to give up teaching and make a full-time commitment to handling the business of the estate. If I don't take charge, the cash worth will simply erode. It would be stupid to let that happen."

"Are you talking about just your share of the estate, or mine as well?" Vicky asked.

"You'll have to make that final choice, of course, but if it's agreeable with you, I'd prefer that we keep everything jointly. We wouldn't weaken the structure of the holdings the way it would be if it were divided. On the other hand, if we keep everything and simply trust it to others to manage without our supervision, we'd be asking for major trouble and probably ultimate financial ruin. Since you live in England, you aren't going to be able to deal with day-to-day matters that come up, but I'm here, and I can. I think we should both learn everything we can. My idea is that I will take charge of all the routine business, but when it comes to major decisions such as buying or selling a piece of property or a really large block of stock, we should confer together as partners. It's easy enough to be in touch frequently by telephone, and when it seems really necessary, you can always make a business trip here. What do you say?"

"There's a tremendous amount of property and investments involved." Vicky was thoughtful. "It seems like a great deal of business for one person to manage. Are you sure this is what you really want to do, Chrissie? You love teaching."

Chrissie nodded. "Yes, I do love teaching, and I'll miss it. Also, I've been afraid of this inheritance and the responsibility that goes with it. I wanted to take the easy way out, but I don't anymore. Our mother left a fortune to us in good faith. Under the circumstances, it was the only legacy she had to offer us. It's up to us to take good care of it, and now I'm prepared to do that."

"I agree with what you're saying, but it doesn't seem fair to you," Vicky replied. "As you said, I'll be in England, out of the fray, while you'll have all the work and headaches. If it's to be a partnership, it would be an uneven one. I wouldn't be carrying my full share of the load."

Bob Raleigh spoke up. "If I may offer my opinion, I think the proposition is an excellent one. One of you should be clearly in charge, and it makes sense that it be Miss Barrows. As she pointed out, she resides in this country, and logistically it will be easier for her to deal with daily events than for you. If it bothers you that she'd be doing most of the work, I suggest you draw up a partnership agreement whereby Miss Barrows is paid an executive salary out of your share of profits."

"Of course. How sensible!" Vicky laughed. She turned to consult her husband. "What do you think about this idea?"

"It's up to you, of course," Paul said. "But I think if Chrissie is willing to take charge, it's the perfect solution. You've been worrying about how you were going to be able to take care of things from London."

Vicky looked at Chrissie once more and nodded. "If you're sure this is what you really want, then you have my approval, as well as my gratitude. I promise to help as much as I can."

They clasped hands, and Chrissie smiled. "As long as we pull together, I'm convinced we'll do fine."

Some of the other men around the table offered their advice and suggestions. As he listened to the flow of conversation surrounding him, Drew was puzzled over Chrissie's complete about-face. From a person who first insisted she wanted nothing whatever from her mother's estate, to a woman who wanted to give it all away to a charity so she wouldn't have to deal with it, it was strange that she was now ready to dedicate all her time and energy to the business of managing the Douglas-Timms holdings. He wondered whether Chrissie really knew her own mind.

It was unfeasible to suppose that his own stringent objections to her abdicating her responsibility might have influenced Chrissie's change of heart. She'd been angry with him when they'd discussed it, and in the end she'd shown him just what she thought of his opinions and his character. Given her view of his motivations, his advice was probably the last she would have accepted.

Drew watched Chrissie speaking to Raleigh at the other end of the long conference table. She was half-turned away, and he was able to observe her profile without her notice. Today she wore a tailored white linen dress topped by a conservative navy-blue jacket. Though she was lovely as always, her appearance was as crisp and businesslike as this new manner of hers. Drew had never seen her this way before—as a determined take-charge individual. Deep inside him, the change sparked a reluctant admiration and grudging respect. Given her prior fears and feelings of inadequacy, it had taken courage.

Still her presence today was painful for him. The day of the Nashes' arrival, he'd been so numb he'd been able to overcome his real feelings about her. Today was another story. The numbness of shock and despair had worn off, giving way to both anger and a vulnerability that unnerved him. Paradoxically he both loved and hated Chrissie.

Somehow, someday, Drew mused unhappily, he was going to have to deal with these conflicting emotions if he was ever to put Chrissie out of mind altogether.

Deep in thought, Drew completely tuned out the others in the room. Unfocused, his eyes were fixed on the blank yellow legal pad on the table before him.

"What do you say to this, Drew?"

At the sound of his own name Drew lifted his head with a start.

Bob Raleigh had spoken to him, and Drew was abruptly conscious that all eyes were upon him. He felt like a small child caught daydreaming in class. "I beg your pardon," he said, chagrined. "I'm afraid I lost track of the conversation. Would you mind repeating what you said?"

"We all agree that Miss Barrows is going to be needing a great deal of legal assistance, especially in the next few months as she learns how to handle the business of the estate."

"Yes?"

"Miss Barrows just made the request that you be placed in complete charge of all her legal interests and be prepared to help and advise her in every way possible. Is this agreeable to you?"

Drew was stunned. His gaze moved swiftly from Raleigh's questioning face to Chrissie's. Her color seemed heightened, but her gaze was steady as she met his eyes and quietly awaited his reply. "But what about John?" Drew was in a turmoil of confusion. "He's the man with a handle on all the financial details of the estate."

"So he is. But Miss Barrows believes she would be more comfortable working with you since she's dealt with you from the beginning. John understands and is agreeable. I presume the matter is acceptable to you, as well?"

Drew was quite aware that Raleigh's last sentence had been more in the nature of a statement rather than a question, but he ignored it. "What about the Wellington case? You know that will soon be taking almost all my time."

Chrissie spoke directly to him for the first time since they'd sat down at the table. "I'm not asking for all your time, Mr. Casey," she said formally. "Only a little of it— whenever I need help understanding some legality or other. I'm not asking that you hold my hand every time I cross the street."

Suddenly Drew was furious. How dare Chrissie put him on the spot like this . . . publicly, in front of his boss and his colleagues! For some reason, she detested him so much that now she was throwing her weight around by putting this new pressure on him. He supposed it was her way of humiliating him by making it impossible for him to refuse. She was showing him that she had power over him whether he liked it or not, that she could snap her fingers, and he was supposed to jump through hoops! But why? Did she have such a mean streak in her that she would find that amusing?

Well! He was nobody's circus dog! By God, he wouldn't meekly submit while she proceeded to destroy every last vestige of his self-respect and pride. He'd thought he loved her, but she had turned into some heartless monster he didn't even know.

"No, thanks," Drew said shortly. He dragged his gaze from Chrissie back to Raleigh, fully aware but beyond caring that his brusque manner was a profound shock to everyone at the table. "I have my hands full as it is. Let John do it."

Raleigh stared at him as though he'd taken leave of his senses. Then the man's anger became plainly visible. He wasn't used to having his orders, even when couched in terms of a polite request, being thwarted by an employee, so Drew was not at all surprised when Raleigh practically roared his angry challenge at him. "And if I insist?"

Drew's blood seemed to turn to ice. "Do you, sir?"

The tension in the room had become palpable.

"I do," Raleigh answered implacably.

Drew inhaled a deep breath through his teeth. Then he shoved back his chair and surged to his feet. "In that case, you'll have to excuse me, sir," he said in a rigidly controlled voice. "I have no choice except to resign my position with the firm, effective immediately."

During the shocked silence that followed, and without a glance toward the woman who had just wrecked his career, Drew walked toward the door, opened it and left the room.

Chapter Ten

A soft knock fell against the door, followed by its opening. At once light from the hallway spilled into the darkened bedroom and illuminated the silhouette in the doorway.

Vicky's concerned voice penetrated the gloom. "Chrissie, are you awake?"

"I'm awake." Chrissie didn't move from her prone position on the bed.

"Alice prepared you a tray, and I brought it up." Juggling the tray with one hand, Vicky flipped on the wall light switch with the other.

As strong light flooded the room and Vicky came to place the tray on the bedside table, Chrissie groaned and crossed her arm over her eyes to shield them from the painful light. "I'm not hungry," she stated in the tone of a pouting child.

"Nonsense." Vicky's voice was bracing. She sat down on the edge of the bed. "You're unhappy, but I won't allow you to starve yourself."

Chrissie drew herself up into a semireclining position, punching the pillows up behind her. "I'm honestly not hungry," she repeated more firmly. "I couldn't possibly eat."

"Then at least drink the tea. It'll make you feel better." Vicky stood up and poured steaming tea from a small silver pot into a cup, liberally laced it with sugar and milk and offered it to her sister.

Chrissie gave in, accepting the cup while she grumbled, "A typical British solution to everything—a cup of tea." She sighed. "If only life were that easy."

"I know it's simplistic," Vicky apologized as she sat down on the bed again, "but it helps. Can something that offers even a shred of comfort be wrong?"

"I suppose not," Chrissie conceded.

"Then drink it while it's hot."

Chrissie obeyed. It was easier than resisting, though she had no faith whatsoever in the restorative powers of a cup of tea. Her life was in shambles, and now she'd ruined Drew's, as well. She saw no way to solve unsolvable problems, and even though sustenance might keep the body in some semblance of normalcy, nothing could help her mentally or emotionally. She was drained.

"The day I arrived you started to tell me there'd been something between you and Drew and that you'd ruined it," Vicky reminded her. "But we were interrupted, and you never mentioned it again and I didn't feel I should pry. I still don't, but I'm ready to listen if you want to talk about it. Do you, Chrissie, or shall I go away and mind my own business?"

Chrissie shook her head. "No. Don't go away. The only reason I changed my mind about confiding in you was because I didn't want to spoil your visit by loading you down with my dreary problems. After what happened this afternoon, though, naturally you're curious. Everyone must be."

It was a massive understatement, Chrissie thought wryly as she took another sip of her tea. Drew's explosion during the meeting had stunned them all, as though someone had dropped a bomb in the middle of the table. His sudden departure had effectively brought the meeting to an end. Or rather, she silently amended, her own inability to continue had ended the meeting. Vaguely Chrissie recalled stumbling to her feet and mumbling that she needed fresh air.

Fortunately Paul Nash had had the presence of mind to see just what bad shape she was in. He'd jumped up from his chair, taken her arm before she could reach the door and wander off, and brusquely told the others the meeting was over. By then Vicky was with her, too, sliding a protective arm around Chrissie's waist. Somehow Vicky and Paul managed to get Chrissie home, though she had no recollection of the journey itself.

When they'd reached the house, Vicky had guided her upstairs to bed. Chrissie realized that many long hours had passed since, because it was dark outside her window. Yet she'd had no awareness of time passing. She hadn't slept, but neither had she had a sense of being consciously awake. She'd been in some strange twilight state where her mind had floated free, allowing her to clearly see and review all that had occurred, without emotional involvement. Chrissie supposed it was her mind's way of coping with stress and unbearable sorrow.

But now that she was sitting up, with full light in the room and a warm drink inside her, she felt more normal. The shock of Drew's unexpected reaction this afternoon was wearing off, and now she felt the full impact of pain and guilt spreading across her entire being.

Chrissie's eyes were bleak as she met her sister's gaze. "I love Drew with all my heart, but all I've ever managed to do is hurt him and anger him. He hates me now." Her voice broke over a sob.

"But...why?" Vicky asked gently. "What have you done?"

"In a terrible way, I doubted his love. Later I tried to talk to him, to apologize for what I realized had been a dreadful mistake. I did my best to convince him that I really love him, but he doesn't believe me. Or rather," she amended sadly, "he doesn't want to believe me." In bald, unadorned words, she outlined exactly what had happened the day of Drew's proposal.

"Ouch!" Vicky exclaimed. "That was a pretty strong condemnation. Knowing how he feels, why did you make that stipulation today that only Drew should work with you on the estate's legal affairs? Were you deliberately trying to needle him, Chrissie, or do you just have a self-destructive urge? Surely you must have realized you were pushing him into a corner and that the only way he could protect himself was to fight back."

"It wasn't like that!" Chrissie cried. "But if you can ask such a question, then that must be exactly what Drew thinks! And all I was really trying to do was to find a way to be with him sometimes. I thought if he was forced to see me and work with me occasionally, eventually he would thaw and forgive me...love me again! I never dreamed I'd drive him to quit his job rather than associate with me! Oh, Vicky, I've really messed things up this time!"

"If you really love Drew as much as you claim, you won't go on hiding out in this room," Vicky said with sudden spirit. "You'll straighten things out."

"How?"

Vicky spread her hands. "That's up to you. But I will say this much—a romantic relationship between you is beside the point. Drew's livelihood is at stake. I think you ought to do something about that."

"Yes," Chrissie replied sadly. "His job and his pride are at stake. I managed to take them both away from him."

Vicky's tone softened. "It's understandable that Drew was crushed when you accused him of only wanting your money. That would have to be a terrible blow to any man's ego when he's proposed marriage to the woman he loves."

"I know." Chrissie was humbled. "I've had a lot of time to reflect on the enormity of what I did. He's the most kindhearted man I ever met, and I hurt him badly. Without even thinking, I did it again today. You're right. I've got to do something to make it up to him. But what? What?"

After a long, sleepless night, Chrissie finally had a plan. Her parents were flying in that morning, but eager as she was to see them, what she had to do was more important than meeting their plane. At breakfast, she delegated the task to Paul and Vicky, who were happy to take it on, and then she set out for Pitts, Smythe and Raleigh.

Bob Raleigh received her immediately, and Chrissie got straight down to business. "I want you to give Drew Casey his job back."

Raleigh nodded somberly. "I'd be happy to do it. Drew's a fine attorney, and I don't want to lose him. But after yesterday, I don't know if I can persuade him to come back. We rather had a run-in ourselves, remember? Besides, even if he did return, he made it plain he won't handle your account."

Chrissie winced. "I'll say he did! As far as I'm concerned, from now on John Keene is in charge of all my legal affairs with this firm. Your run-in with Drew yesterday was all my fault, Bob. I pushed him too hard by requesting that he handle my account. I had my reasons, but it just didn't work out. When you backed me up by trying to order him to work with me, Drew really didn't have any choice but to refuse...even to quit. I hope you won't hold that against him if he wants to come back."

Raleigh grinned, suddenly enlightened. "I got caught in the crossfires of a lover's quarrel, didn't I?"

Chrissie's own smile was wan. "It's a little more serious than that," she admitted. "I don't believe there can ever be anything between us now, but I did Drew a great injustice, and now I'm trying to set things right so far as I can. I can't bear to live with the responsibility of causing him to lose a job he loves."

Raleigh nodded and reached toward the telephone. "I'll call him now, if you like, and see what he has to say about coming back."

Chrissie forestalled him, placing her own hand across the receiver before Raleigh could lift it. "I'd appreciate it if you'd let me be the one to tell him in my own way. It's my fault he walked out, and it's up to me to persuade him to return. I just had to know if it was all right with you."

"Fine." Raleigh gave her shoulder a fatherly pat. "I'll leave it to you, then. Tell him I'd like him back here first thing Monday morning. As for the trouble between the two of you—good luck to you."

"Thanks," Chrissie replied huskily.

After she left the law office, she drove to the mall where Drew's mother worked as a manager in a department store. She had telephoned Maggie at home early that morning, and they had arranged to meet for lunch.

In the coffee shop inside the mall, the two women ordered their food, and then Maggie looked at Chrissie with knowing eyes. "This isn't a social visit," she stated flatly. "Something's bothering you, and it has to do with my son, or you wouldn't have called me. What is it?"

"I need your help, Maggie," Chrissie said frankly. "I want to ask a favor."

Drew got out of his car and walked up the sidewalk to his mother's house, adjusting his tie as he went. In the driveway were two cars he recognized as belonging to his brothers, but another car parked at the curb was unfamiliar.

Maggie had been mysterious on the telephone the night before when she'd called to issue a dinner invitation. "Wear a suit and tie," she'd instructed. "It's a special occasion." But she'd refused to elaborate on the reason for the gathering, and Drew was still trying to puzzle it out. It wasn't the birthday or anniversary of anybody in the family.

As far as he was concerned, his mother's "special occasion" couldn't have come at a worse time. Ever since he'd so abruptly quit his job two days ago, his disposition had been grim. He was in no mood to socialize with anyone, not even his own family.

Drew felt the loss of his job keenly, yet even now it seemed the only possible thing he could have and preserved even the smallest thread of dignity. He couldn't have gone on respecting himself if he'd caved in to Chrissie's demands about personally handling her legal account. She'd been presumptuous and manipulative, but he'd shown her that no matter what she thought or wanted, he did not have to play her game. He was the one in charge of his own life, not her.

But his pride was of small comfort. He was now without a job. That was bad enough, but he was also without the woman he couldn't stop loving even after all Chrissie's cruelties. Drew marveled that body, mind and soul, he could still long for Chrissie at the same time that he hated her! His was a pitiful case indeed!

When he reached the door, Drew did not ring the bell. None of the brothers ever did. He simply opened it and stepped inside the entrance hall. From the living room came the babble of many voices.

Drew walked toward the living room and paused for a moment in the doorway. His gaze traveled around the room, taking in the people there, and all at once the breath was knocked out of him. There stood Chrissie chatting with one of his sisters-in-law.

She looked stunning. She wore a shimmering white dress that exposed her apricot-pink shoulders and throat. Her beautiful fiery hair was silky, cascading down her back in waves of glory. Her profile was delicate, exquisitely molded, and for a long moment his gaze rested on the fine details of her face and throat before finally taking in the fullness of her breasts, the incredibly narrow waist, the trim, sensuously curved hips, the length of her legs beneath the long, narrow skirt of her dress. She had never appeared more enchanting, and Drew's blood began to race.

What was Chrissie doing here in his mother's house? And all the others? Drew recognized Paul and Vicky Nash, of course, along with the members of his own family, but there was another, older couple present he had never seen before. Why had his mother taken it upon herself to invite these people . . . Chrissie . . . to dinner? Especially now?

Drew's first instinct was to turn on his heels and leave quickly before anyone spotted him. He very nearly did just that, but then he knew he could not. There'd been enough walking away from Chrissie already—the day he'd proposed, the day of the conference meeting. He'd had valid reasons to leave both times, but this was different. This was *his* territory—*his* mother's home. He didn't know what the hell Chrissie was doing here, but he was damned if he'd be driven away. She had already pushed him to ultimate limits, but here and now it ended. He wouldn't be pushed anymore.

"Hello, everyone," he said in a loud, cheerful voice that demanded attention. "What a surprise! Mother, precisely what *is* the nature of this supersecret special occasion?"

Maggie hurried to his side, smiling as she took his arm. Her fingers pressed hard into his coat sleeve. "Chrissie's parents are here from New Orleans. We thought it would be nice to welcome them to California with a family dinner party.''

Left unsaid was how she had come to be involved with Chrissie...or why she'd considered it necessary to lump the Casey family with the Barrows family as though they all belonged together. Drew gave his mother a long look, and she stared back, seemingly guileless. But lurking in the depths of her eyes was a silent warning that plainly said he was not to rock any boats by fishing for too many details.

Drew was almost amused at the suggestion of panic in his mother's normally tranquil face. She was genuinely nervous over what his reaction might be...as well she should be! Maggie had entered into some sort of conspiracy with Chrissie, the last person in the world he wanted to see. By his mother's meddling, he was now placed in the uncomfortable position of having to be sociable to Chrissie's entire family in the midst of his own. It was an unspeakable act of treason on his mother's part, and by the slight pressure of her fingers on his arm, he knew she was well aware of her treachery and was fearful of his possible response.

''Did you now?'' Drew drawled in a pleasant noncommittal reply to his mother's statement. The words sounded harmless enough, but he saw that Maggie had caught the challenge behind them. He wasn't buying his mother's fabrication for a second, and she knew it.

Maggie's smile grew strained, and her fingers dug harder into his arm. ''Come meet Chrissie's parents,'' she urged. Beneath the suggestion was a stern maternal order to behave, the secret language that begins early between every mother and child, yet Drew could tell that this time Maggie was uncertain her silent command would be heeded.

He almost laughed aloud. Maggie was definitely squirming, and it served her right! Even so, he chose to be gracious and not embarrass her...yet. Drew wasn't certain exactly what was going on here, so he mentally reserved the right to make a nasty scene later if he saw fit.

Pulling his abused arm from his mother's clutches, Drew stepped forward and introduced himself to the Barrows with perfect cordiality. Next, he spoke to the Nashes, again with an easy grace that belied the tension inside him. His greeting to his brothers and their wives was more offhanded, but no less warm. Finally there was no further excuse to avoid Chrissie.

He turned, and Chrissie's face visibly paled as he approached her. It did his heart good to note her unease. God, the woman had incredible nerve, bringing her entire family to his mother's house after all she'd done to him! Her gall infuriated him, but mindful of a roomful of people who could overhear their every word, Drew kept his hostility carefully concealed.

"Good evening, Chrissie," he said, scrupulously polite.

"Hello, Drew. It's good to see you again. How...how are you?" Despite her extreme nervousness, which was readily apparent to him as he stepped close to her, she returned his greeting with only the slightest overt evidence of tension. She was a good actress, he had to acknowledge that. Drew doubted if anyone else in the room could tell how rigid her smile was, how uptight she seemed.

"Oh, I'm fine," he replied with the ghost of a smile. "Really fine. Everything's just wonderful with me these days."

Drew's tone was agreeable enough. No possible fault could be found in his urbane manner, but Chrissie wasn't fooled. She hadn't missed the edge of heavy sarcasm in his answer to her question. He was positively livid that she was here, that she and Maggie had tricked him into seeing her this evening. She could tell that by the ugly twist to his smile and the frostiness in his gaze.

Her heart sank, and yet Drew's reaction to her presence was exactly what she'd expected, so it wasn't a surprise. She'd known perfectly well that he wouldn't be glad to see her. Not that she could blame him for that, given the circumstances. Considering everything, she supposed she ought to count herself fortunate that he hadn't made a scene and physically tossed her out of the house. It was going to be sheer hell to get through dinner and carry out her plan, but she was determined to do it. She owed Drew, after all. And anyway, what she had planned was little enough as it was. What did it matter whether she was uncomfortable or not? After tonight, she would never see Drew again. No, she would simply grit her teeth and carry on for now.

Maggie joined them. "Drew, would you like a drink before dinner?"

Clearly his mother was coming to rescue Chrissie, like a mother bear coming to the aid of her cub. Only in this case Maggie had turned her back on her own flesh-and-blood cub and rushed in to assist the enemy cub! When this evening was over, Drew decided grimly, his mother was going to have a lot of explaining to do, and it had damned well better be good. Never in a million years would he have dreamed his own mother would turn on him like this!

"No, thanks," he replied shortly.

"Then we'll go ahead and serve dinner. Everyone else has already finished their drinks."

"It would seem that they were invited to arrive earlier than I was," Drew said as he pointedly glanced at his watch. "You told me eight o'clock, and it's now five after."

"Did I?" Maggie asked nervously. "So sorry, darling. I must have made a mistake about the time when I spoke to you."

"Hmm." Drew simply looked at her.

Maggie glanced away. "Chrissie, would you help me carry in the salad?" she asked in an effort to change the subject. "And Drew, I'd appreciate it if you'd fill the wineglasses."

Dinner was a lively, pleasant affair with good food and interesting conversation. Chrissie noted how well her family got on with Drew's family. It might have been more gratifying if she had any hope about her own relationship with Drew, but she had driven a permanent wedge between them and she had finally accepted it in the deepest part of her heart. What was over was over.

Drew sat at the head of the table, opposite Maggie, and from her position at the center, Chrissie stole covert glances at him as he chatted with her mother. She was memorizing the way he looked just now, so that she could think back to this moment during the bleak drought ahead. She would always be able to hold Drew in her mind and heart, remembering the exact shape of his head, the sparkle in his eyes and the way his mouth crooked whenever he smiled. At least nobody could deny her that.

Alternately it seemed as though the meal dragged on with endless slowness or flew past on wings. Chrissie longed for nothing so much as for the evening to be over, but she dreaded what lay immediately ahead. Drew was so unpredictable, so angry with her that he might humiliate her before both their families. Yet it was a chance she had to take. She had chosen this public way of confronting him and being able to speak to him because she couldn't think of any other way to get him to listen to her. Certainly if she'd attempted to go to his apartment to talk to him, he would have snubbed her. And anyway, what she had to say needed to be spoken in front of others if she wanted to restore his wounded pride before she got out of his life for good.

When they reached the coffee and dessert stage and everyone had been served, Maggie tapped her wineglass to

gain attention and then announced, "Chrissie has something she wishes to say to us."

Chrissie's throat constricted now that the moment had
actually come. She swallowed painfully, removed the narrow gift box from beneath the napkin on her lap and slowly
rose to her feet.

She carefully kept her eyes averted from Drew as she began to speak. "On Monday my stay in Los Angeles will
come to an end. I'll be heading back to Louisiana with my
parents, and Vicky and Paul will go back to England. Although estate business will bring me back here from time to
time, it will probably only be for short trips with a busy
schedule, and unlike this first time, I won't be feeling so lost
and lonely as I was when I first arrived. So..." Chrissie
smiled as she glanced around the table. "I want to thank the
Casey clan for befriending me when I needed friendship and
acceptance during a difficult period in my life."

"Here, here!" Bruce Casey chuckled and applauded. The
others joined in.

When they were silent once more, Chrissie continued. "I
especially want to thank Maggie for extending understanding to me when she would have been justified in turning a
cold shoulder to me. Without her generosity and kindness,
I couldn't be speaking to you all right now." She glanced at
Maggie, who smiled and nodded encouragingly.

"Next, I want to thank my parents for being so loving and
supportive to me all my life. No girl, adopted or not, could
ever ask for a better family, and I know how fortunate I
am." Marie smiled at Chrissie, while Jack raised a thumbs-
up sign of approval.

Chrissie went on. "I'd like to thank Vicky simply for
being herself. Words can't express my joy in meeting my
twin sister. It's the most wonderful gift I've ever received,
and so I must also pay a tribute to our birth mother, Laura
Douglas, for seeing to it that we were finally brought to-

gether. I look forward to a growing closeness between us for the rest of our lives." Vicky blew her a silent kiss, and then Chrissie smiled at Paul. "I want to thank you, Paul, for so warmly accepting me within your family circle. You might have resented my sudden intrusion into your lives, but you chose instead to become a real brother to me, as well as my sister's husband. Now if only you'd refrain from snapping pictures all the time...!"

Everyone chuckled as Paul snapped his fingers and pretended to jump up from his chair. "That reminds me! I left my camera in the car!"

The lighthearted moment eased the tension within Chrissie for a brief instant, long enough so that she could take a deep breath before she went on. Then she picked up the small white gift package from the table and, working up her courage, looked along the table to Drew. She forced herself to meet his eyes, and he was gazing at her with an intense, thoughtful frown.

To the table at large, Chrissie said, "As for Drew, I owe him an enormous debt of gratitude. He came to New Orleans to tell me about my inheritance and brought me the stupendous news that I had an identical twin sister. Then he set the wheels in motion to locate her." Speaking to him directly for the first time, she said softly and earnestly, "I can never, ever thank you enough for that...for bringing us together."

"That goes for me, too," Vicky interjected.

"It was my pleasure." Drew managed a smile as the group around the table applauded again, but his lips felt stiff and his whole body was taut. He wasn't in the least mollified by Chrissie's tribute. Somehow he knew that wasn't all Chrissie had to say to him, and he tensed as he waited for the rest of it. If she was about to tell the whole bunch of them how she'd humiliated him, he would strangle her!

"I was under a tremendous amount of stress when I first arrived in Los Angeles," Chrissie added now. "Besides the anxiety over locating Vicky, I was in shock over learning that Laura Douglas was my birth mother and that she'd left me a fortune. Then the responsibility for so much money terrified me, and I was intimidated by having to deal with a group of attorneys. I was in over my head and I knew it, but Drew somehow managed to make everything as painless as possible. He explained things in a way I could understand, advised me and on occasion even lectured me when I needed it. He went out of his way to help me. In return, I..." Here, for the first time, Chrissie's voice broke. "In return for all of the kind, thoughtful things Drew did for me, I paid him back with a terrible injustice and I... now I just want to set the record straight and make things right as far as I am able." Sucking in a quick breath, Chrissie addressed him directly once more. "I'm sorry," she said huskily. "Please accept this small gift as a token of my esteem and with my deepest apologies."

The gift was passed down the table as Chrissie sat down again. She realized she was trembling and suddenly chilled.

Drew accepted the gift with trepidation. He wanted nothing from Chrissie, especially not her apologies. At least, he consoled himself as he tore away the white wrapping paper, she hadn't embarrassed him by airing their dirty linen in front of their families. She'd admitted she'd done him an injury, but she hadn't been specific. He was grateful that she'd spared him that.

The box contained a sterling silver pen and pencil set with his engraved initials. It was precisely the right sort of gift a woman could give a man who'd been a business associate without raising eyebrows—a fine gift, but with no overtones of intimacy. But the real gift Chrissie had given him was not the writing implements themselves, but the handwritten note Drew found inside the box.

It read: "Raleigh expects you back at work Monday morning. No strings. I will forever regret hurting you, but I will never regret always loving you. Be happy. Goodbye, Chrissie."

Chrissie had tried to apologize to him once before, to tell him that she loved him, but Drew had been too stubborn, too angry and hurt to listen. He'd been angry tonight, too, right up to the bitter end of her little speech. But now, all at once, the hard feelings were gone. He realized that by coming here tonight—to his home—and saying the things she'd said in front of the others, Chrissie had been setting herself up for the possibility of the humiliation of his rejection. She had wanted to convey to him publicly just how much she valued him, yet she'd been prudent and careful in her words. She'd refrained from mentioning her rebuff to his marriage proposal or even the fact that he'd quit his job in a huff because of her. Drew realized with a sudden shock that she'd made the speech she had, had kept silent about details, to *protect his pride*!

And now this note. Obviously Chrissie had talked with Raleigh about giving him back his job, and as for the rest of it . . .

". . . I will never regret always loving you . . ."

Damned if he knew why, given the cold way he'd treated her. Drew carefully pocketed the note as he lifted his head and looked across the table at Chrissie. Even from a distance he could see the dark anxiety haunting her eyes. She didn't know what to expect from him. With shame, Drew realized she had a valid reason for her fear, the way he'd been erupting into a blind fury these days. Yet she said she still loved him. The words melted the ice surrounding his heart, and flames of warmth radiated through him.

Abruptly Drew shoved back his chair, and he walked around the table to stand behind Chrissie. She looked sur-

prised and wary, but she didn't resist when he took her hand
and helped her out of her chair.

When she was standing facing him, with her hand still
tightly clasped in his, Drew looked deeply into her eyes. But
his words were addressed to her parents especially and, more
generally, to the room at large. "Mr. and Mrs. Barrows,
you'll have to excuse us now. I intend to take this lady away
somewhere private so that I can ask her to marry me."

He heard Chrissie's quick intake of breath. Drew's entire
body seemed to be melting now in the glow of the love that
had spread through him. He smiled tenderly at Chrissie and
asked in a whisper, "Is that all right with you?"

Chrissie's head bobbed up and down. For an instant she
couldn't seem to speak. Unexpected happiness clogged her
throat. The loving expression in Drew's eyes was so deep, so
immense it seemed to draw her soul right into his own heart.

"Yes," she heard herself answering. "Oh, Drew, yes, yes,
yes!"

Drew pulled her within the circle of his embrace. Ignoring the excited murmur of voices and fresh applause coming from the table, he bent his head to kiss the love of his
life—the woman who would be his bride. Their lips met in
a warmth that was like honey, thick and sweet and soothing. The nightmare of being apart was over at last.

A minute later, laughing, they started for the door, but
Jack Barrow's commanding voice stopped them. "Andrew, does this mean my daughter won't be going home with
us on Monday?"

As they both turned back to face the group at the table,
Drew replied, "Yes, sir. It means exactly that."

"What about the wedding?" Marie asked Chrissie,
round-eyed. "You'll come home and let me help you plan
your wedding, won't you?"

"What about us?" Vicky wailed. "You can't let us go back to London and then have a wedding without me there!"

Maggie's eyes twinkled as she chimed in, addressing her son. "What about me? Have you forgiven me enough to *invite* me to the wedding?"

Drew chuckled. "You're forgiven, Mom, and yes, you'll be invited to the wedding. As to the rest of your questions, we'll give you our answer tomorrow. We're going now," he added firmly, "so we can set the date."

For the first time since Drew's unexpected proposal, Chrissie addressed the group at large. "I can promise you all this much at least . . . the wedding will be *soon*." The last word was spoken as Drew impatiently pulled her out of the room and out of the house.

In the concealing dark shadow of a tree, Drew kissed Chrissie again, this time in a manner that was thoroughly satisfying to them both.

At last, breathless and shaken, the words came. "I love you, Chrissie," Drew murmured. "Even when I tried to hate you, I loved you. Makes no sense, does it?" he asked with a wry smile.

"Makes perfect sense to me. I love you, too, Drew, so very much. I did the day I drove you away from me. But I was so afraid about everything . . . the money . . . the responsibility and . . . and then when you proposed out of the blue like that, so suddenly . . ."

"I know. I've had time to see why you were wary about it. We'd known each other so briefly. You really didn't know anything about me. But believe me, darling, it was never your money I wanted. I've got plenty for my own needs, enough to support a family—now that I've got my job back anyway," he added, chuckling. "I only wanted you, always, from the first night I met you when you let me come in from the rain."

"Truly?"

"Truly. As for your inheritance, I simply didn't want to see you throw it away. I just didn't think that was fair to Laura's memory or to the people who now depend on you for their jobs."

"You were right, of course." Chrissie sighed. "The day of the conference meeting, when I got so high-handed about naming you to handle the estate business, it was only so that I'd have the opportunity to get near you again, to try to make you listen to me and understand how sorry I was to have doubted you. Can you really forgive me for everything?"

"I can try." Drew grinned, then kissed the corner of her mouth. "Did you really mean what you said back there—that you want us to be married soon?"

Chrissie nodded, and her eyes were shining. "The sooner the better," she said, echoing Drew's words that first day he'd proposed. Then she sighed. "Unfortunately, that will make my mother unhappy. She's always wanted to give me a big New Orleans-style wedding—the kind that takes about a year to put together."

"She won't get it," Drew said firmly, "but maybe we can come up with something that will please her and everybody else. Come on," he added urgently as he tugged her hands once more. "Let's go to my place. If we want to make all those people back there in the house happy, we've got to get to work planning our wedding."

Chrissie halted. "Is that the very *first* thing we have to do?"

Drew laughed huskily and gave her a hug. "You little devil! Well . . . maybe not the very first thing. . . ."

*   *   *   *   *

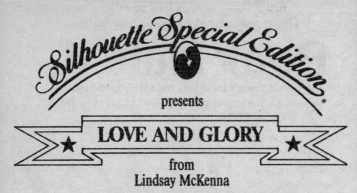

Silhouette Special Edition

presents

LOVE AND GLORY

from
Lindsay McKenna

Introducing a gripping new series celebrating our men—and women—in uniform. Meet the Trayherns, a military family as proud and colorful as the American flag, a family fighting the shadow of dishonor, a family determined to triumph—with **LOVE AND GLORY!**

June: **A QUESTION OF HONOR** (SE #529) leads the fast-paced excitement. When Coast Guard officer Noah Trayhern offers Kit Anderson a safe house, he unwittingly endangers his own guarded emotions.

July: **NO SURRENDER** (SE #535) Navy pilot Alyssa Trayhern's assignment with arrogant jet jockey Clay Cantrell threatens her career—and her heart—with a crash landing!

August: **RETURN OF A HERO** (SE #541) Strike up the band to welcome home a man whose top-secret reappearance will make headline news . . . with a delicate, daring woman by his side.

Three courageous siblings—
three consecutive months of

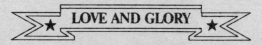

LOVE AND GLORY

Premiering in **June**, only in
Silhouette Special Edition.

You'll flip . . . your pages won't!
Read paperbacks *hands-free* with

Book Mate •I

The perfect "mate" for all your romance paperbacks

**Traveling • Vacationing • At Work • In Bed • Studying
• Cooking • Eating**

Perfect size for all standard paperbacks, this wonderful invention makes reading a pure pleasure! Ingenious design holds paperback books OPEN and FLAT so even wind can't ruffle pages — leaves your hands free to do other things. Reinforced, wipe-clean vinyl-covered holder flexes to let you turn pages without undoing the strap . . . supports paperbacks so well, they have the strength of hardcovers!

Pages turn WITHOUT opening the strap.

SEE·THROUGH STRAP

Reinforced back stays flat.

Built in bookmark

BOOK MARK

BACK COVER HOLDING STRIP

10˝ x 7¼˝. opened.
Snaps closed for easy carrying, too.

FOUR UNIQUE SERIES
FOR EVERY WOMAN YOU ARE...

Silhouette Romance

Love, at its most tender, provocative,
emotional... in stories that will make you laugh and
cry while bringing you the magic of falling in love.

6 titles per month

Silhouette Special Edition

Sophisticated, substantial and packed with
emotion, these powerful novels of life and love will
capture your imagination and steal your heart.

6 titles per month

Silhouette Desire

Open the door to romance and passion. Humorous,
emotional, compelling—yet always a believable
and sensuous story—Silhouette Desire never
fails to deliver on the promise of love.

6 titles per month

Silhouette Intimate Moments

Enter a world of excitement, of romance
heightened by suspense, adventure and the
passions every woman dreams of. Let us
sweep you away.

4 titles per month

Silhouette Romance®

COMING NEXT MONTH

#652 THE ENCHANTED SUMMER—Victoria Glenn
When Derek Randall was sent to Green Meadow to buy the rights to
the "Baby Katy" doll, he found himself more interested in rights
holder Katy Kruger—a real live doll herself!

#653 AGELESS PASSION, TIMELESS LOVE—
Phyllis Halldorson
CEO Courtney Forrester had always discouraged office romances at
his plant. But Assistant Personnel Manager Kirsten Anderson was
proof that rules were meant to be broken....

#654 HIS KIND OF WOMAN—Pat Tracy
As the widow of his boyhood rival, Grace Banner was certainly not
Matthew Hollister's kind of woman...until a passionate battle led
Matthew to a tender change of heart.

#655 TREASURE HUNTERS—Val Whisenand
When Lori Kendall became a contestant on a TV game show she
discovered that the only prize worth winning was teammate Jason
Daniels. But would Jason's secret send Lori home empty-handed?

#656 IT TAKES TWO—Joan Smith
As concierge of an upscale Montreal hotel, Jennie Longman was used
to catering to her guests' eccentric whims. But Wes Adler had a
request that wasn't in Jennie's handbook. He wanted her!

#657 TEACH ME—Stella Bagwell
When secretary Bernadette Baxter started teaching her boss, Nicholas
Atwood, the fine art of dating, she was soon wishing she was the
woman who'd reap the benefits of her lessons....

AVAILABLE THIS MONTH